D1521733

LOVE AND
DEATH IN
CHARLESTON

LOVE AND DEATH IN CHARLESTON

•

Patricia Robinson

AVALON BOOKS
THOMAS BOUREGY AND COMPANY, INC.
401 LAFAYETTE STREET
NEW YORK, NEW YORK 10003

PRINTED IN THE UNITED STATES OF AMERICA
ON ACID-FREE PAPER
BY HADDON CRAFTSMEN, BLOOMSBURG, PENNSYLVANIA

LOVE AND DEATH IN CHARLESTON

Chapter One

Pryor never had been on a plane before. Actually she'd never been beyond Overton, Pennsylvania, before. She sat stiffly in her aisle seat, smoothing the pale blue skirt of the suit that had cost far too much. She was glad her ticket had been sent to her.

Once again she wondered why all this couldn't have been done by mail. The letter from attorney Winthrop J. Hazzard had stunned rather than delighted her. She'd been named in her Aunt Althea's will, which was to be read on October 16 in a house on Tradd Street in Charleston, South Carolina.

She knew none of her Charleston relatives.

1

Her mother had cut herself off from them when she eloped with a violinist from an orchestra on tour. Igor Dimitri had been a charmer, apparently. Alida Amory, a willful, impulsive girl of nineteen, had married him and managed to see Atlanta, Richmond, and New York and get pregnant before he died of flu in another seedy hotel on Third Avenue. Penniless, unskilled, and depressed, Alida, cast into outer darkness by her Charleston kin, went to live with Igor's two sisters in Overton. It was here that Pryor grew up, tended by Bella and Katia Dimitri.

Pryor had good memories of them in their shabby house, where wonderful Russian dishes were cooked and musician friends came every Sunday to play together. It was a cozy, uneventful life until Pryor was eighteen. She was spending the night at her friend Evelyn Johnson's when the little house caught fire and burned to the ground, taking Alida, Bella, and Katia with it.

She stared at the man next to her, wondering about his life. He was handsome, wore an expensive suit, and carried a prestigious-looking briefcase. But his face was tight with strain. He took frequent sips from a silver pocket flask.

At the moment, he was eyeing her appraisingly. She further stiffened, although she felt good about herself. She was glad that she'd had her red-blond hair cut in a neat pageboy, that she was bolstered not only by the blue polyester suit but simulated alligator pumps and matching purse. She took a final sip of her coffee and ignored the man. He had drunk none of his coffee. The Styrofoam cup sat on the tray, pulled out to hold it.

When the stewardess came by, Pryor was ready to hand her an empty cup. The man, fumbling with his flask, reached for his full cup, grasped it, and in handing it to the stewardess, managed to spill its dark contents directly on Pryor's new blue suit.

For a moment she couldn't move. She was aware of the man trying to blot up the disaster with his handkerchief, of the stewardess doing likewise with paper napkins. The people around them were exclaiming noisily. Then the stewardess was heading her down the aisle to the restroom. Water and paper towels did little to pale the dark stain on her jacket and skirt. Finally, she assured the stewardess that all had been done that could be done, that the airline was not guilty, and that all would be well.

All would *not* be well. During the ensuing miles to Charleston, the man slept. Pryor sat as if wishing she could be thrown away. The other passengers stared at her with pity during the disembarking. Standing in the baggage area, waiting for her suitcase, she felt abandoned.

The letter said she would be met at the airport. Other people greeted family or friends and embraced. No one approached Pryor Dimitri. Plucking her suitcase from the carousel of luggage, she stood in her badly stained clothes, looking around helplessly.

Finally a tall, stunning black woman approached her.

"Pryor Dimitri?" The voice was low and cultivated, with just a trace of a Southern accent.

Pryor nodded. "I'm Egypt McDowell. In case you're stunned by my name, alternatives were Ginza or Odessa. I'll take you into town." She picked up the battered suitcase and, followed by Pryor, went to the front of the airport, where a dark green Mercedes waited discreetly.

They sat in the front seat and, though Egypt didn't speak at once, she turned and smiled at Pryor several times. She was quite beautiful, her clothes tasteful but expensive, her manner assured. At last she spoke.

"The others will be waiting at the house," she explained. Her eyes took in Pryor's damaged suit.

"An accident on the plane," Pryor murmured. "I was sitting next to a drunk."

Egypt laughed briefly. "Just brazen it out, my dear."

"Whose house?"

"Your late Aunt Althea's. In case you're wondering about me, my mother worked for your aunt for years. Ma will be around to help out."

They didn't speak again for several miles, gliding down a highway flanked by trees and distant marshes. Finally, Pryor couldn't contain herself.

"I really don't know why I'm here, why I was named in the will. I never knew Althea Amory."

"She knew all about you. Private detective. She was devoted to your mother."

"A private detective?" echoed Pryor.

"Typical of your aunt. She had to know everything about you. Your love life, your income, your friends."

"But why?"

"She was devoted to your mother, her little sister. She admired Alida's gumption, envied her, perhaps. The other person she was devoted to was Rose, her daughter, whom she adored. Rose never married, messed up her life with men and booze, then disappeared; she hasn't been seen in years. I think she's dead. Althea had two other daughters whom you'll meet.''

''Dead?''

''If she were alive Rose would be hanging around, angling for Althea's money.''

''Men, booze, greed—she sounds awful.''

''She was a real charmer, full of joie de vivre. She always could make Althea laugh. She was affectionate and very beautiful.''

''Oh.''

''If you're wondering how I know so much, I was Althea's friend. My mother was her servant and her companion. Althea put me through law school.''

''I see.'' She didn't really.

''Quite a cast of characters. The present cast of characters includes Althea's two other daughters and their husbands. Miranda Garner, the oldest, also beautiful, but sly and a bit conniving. Her husband Bruce, attractive, socially impeccable, devoted to the good things in life. That leaves Linda, the mouse. No one could ever figure why Cleve Martin married her. He was the town prince, so to say. Maybe it was her prospect of money.''

''Aunt Althea had money?''

''Bundles. Some from her father, a lot from

her husband, a Yankee from Detroit; he died young.''

They were crossing a long bridge over a river. Pryor could see a few tall buildings, and church spires, but no skyscrapers. Sailboats drifted on the river.

''Where do you live?'' Pryor asked.

''North Charleston, up there to the left.'' They had entered the peninsula and in minutes were passing street after street of gorgeous eighteenth-and nineteenth-century houses— blue, pale pink, ecru, unpainted brick. The streets were narrow, especially Tradd with its colorful old homes.

''It's so beautiful.'' Pryor had never seen its like. She thought of Overton, a mill town with row after row of drab dwellings and only a few attractive places on the outskirts.

They stopped in front of a large brick house, two rooms wide and three stories high. A large wrought-iron gate led to a garden. Egypt ig- nored the massive brass knocker on a door topped by an exquisitely carved pediment. She took out a key.

In seconds they stood in a vast hall flanked by four doors.

''They're probably in the library,'' said Egypt.

She lead Pryor up a graceful staircase that faced the front door, past what appeared to be family portraits and one or two watercolors of ocean and marsh.

In a smaller hallway, they heard the sound of voices and Egypt proceeded to the farthest door. When she opened it, Pryor felt thrust into a British novel. Two walls of books, leather-covered furniture, and French doors leading to what appeared to be a balcony.

"Egypt! Come in." A tall, incredibly handsome man beckoned to them. "And this must be Pryor. I'm Winthrop Hazzard." He walked from in front of the fireplace and shook hands with Pryor. "Sit down, my dear." He escorted her to a chair next to one of the sofas on either side of the fireplace. "These are your cousins and cousins-in-law, Miranda and Bruce Garner and Linda and Cleve Martin."

Pryor sat, conscious only of her stained suit, the stylish clothes of Linda and Miranda, and the communal stare which proclaimed her dowdiness. Egypt sat at a desk by a window, trying to suppress a smile of amusement.

"Now," said Winthrop Hazzard, holding out a document, "we can get on with the business at hand."

In a low, educated voice, he began. Pryor

heard little. She was entranced by his voice, his perfect features, and his prematurely gray hair, not to mention his suit, shirt, and tie. She stared at his shoes, wondering if the whole ensemble came from London.

He stopped suddenly. ''Look,'' he said, ''if any of you wish to read this, you're welcome. But I think you all prefer that I skip the whereases and herebys and get down to brass tacks.'' He seemed to be steeling himself, took a deep breath, and turned a page. ''Both Sylvia and Egypt McDowell are to get ten thousand dollars each. Five thousand is to go to Jacob Murray, the gardener, twenty thousand to Althea's church, St. Philip's. To her daughters, Linda and Miranda, Althea wills fifty thousand dollars each. The remainder of her estate— holdings of approximately three million dollars, the house, furnishings, and car—are to go to her niece, Pryor Dimitri.''

There was a hush, a long hush, followed suddenly by a cacophony of voices. Pryor heard only bits of the exclamations.

''A nobody.''

''Althea never even knew her.''

''Another lawyer.''

''We can always take it to court.''

''Althea was out of her senses!''

"Senile!"

"Please!" Winthrop Hazzard's voice was commanding. He willed them to silence. "I'll remind you that this document was witnessed by a judge and old Bishop Hatfield. I know it's hard to comprehend Althea's wishes, but they are legal and irrevocable."

The cacophony started again. Winthrop Hazzard walked from the room. One by one they rose, brushed by Pryor, and followed him. They glanced at her as if sighting Coke cans and McDonald's wrappers in the garden of Versailles.

Pryor sat as if nailed to the chair. Finally Egypt pulled her to her feet. "I'll show you your bedroom and then we'll go down and get some supper. Ma's busy in the kitchen. Jacob will bring up your bag."

Pryor followed obediently, too numb to comment. She tried to take in the reality of three million dollars, plus this house.

"It's all for real," said Egypt, opening a door. "I know it's a staggering contrast to your old life, but with time you'll settle in."

It was another incredible room, dominated by a canopied bed with a blue satin cover. The pale blue was echoed in long draperies, a chaise longue, and two side chairs. A huge pier glass dominated the far end of the room. A nicely faded Chinese rug covered most of the wide floorboards.

"You haven't seen anything yet." Egypt took her arm.

They entered a vast walk-in closet with clothes rods on either side. The back of the door was covered by a cloth shoe holder, filled and glowing with all types of footwear. On the poles were more clothes than Pryor ever had seen outside a department store. There were suits and dresses of all colors, skirts and blouses, coats and capes, a shelf of purses.

"Your summer wear is in the guest room," explained Egypt. "Underwear and sweaters are in the bureau."

Pryor touched the sleeve of a jacket. "In a minute I'll wake up and come to my senses."

"All these things are your size," observed Egypt. "The detective again. Look, you're awfully pale. You want to lie down for a bit?"

Pryor walked back into the room. "I should give it all to Linda and Miranda. No matter how Althea felt about them, they were her daughters."

"They never had any feeling for her, nor she for them. Of course, she spoiled them when they were little, a mistake that produced selfish beasts. They couldn't wait for her to die. She loved only her daughter Rose and your mother. Rose, who brought light and laughter and true affection into her life. But then Rose is gone.''

''Where could she be?''

''It's my opinion that she's dead.'' Egypt looked at her directly. ''And not by natural causes.''

Pryor shivered. ''How they all must hate me.''

''That's putting it mildly.''

A slender woman of indeterminate age greeted them in a cheerful kitchen. ''Ma, this is Pryor Dimitri,'' said Egypt. ''Sylvia McDowell, Pryor.''

The setting sun poured through two windows above the copper sink. Copper pots and pans gleamed from hooks on the pale green wall. A long table with chairs stretched down the middle of the room.

It was obvious that Sylvia, despite her regal bearing, had been crying. Egypt put her arms around her. ''Ma, you deserve it. All those years with Althea! Think what you can do with ten thousand dollars! A trip! A new refrigerator! A microwave oven!''

''I'd rather have Althea back.''

''I know, darlin'.''

They ate at the kitchen table, okra gumbo, chicken salad, hot biscuits.

It was between the salad and dessert that Pryor stared at the two elegant black women, watched the room spin and slowly slid to the floor.

Chapter Two

She awoke to darkness, saw by the clock on the bedside table that it was two-thirty. She tried to sleep again, but the events of the day weighed heavily on her. To avoid them she made herself think of Overton, Pennsylvania. Few people had ever heard of it. With a population of about three thousand, it rose modestly on the banks of the dirty Monongahela River, which snaked through the hills toward Pittsburgh. On one side was the railroad and a few isolated homes. On the other squatted more homes, most of them built in the twenties. Pryor's aunts' house was older, a Victorian ruin in need of repair but maintaining a certain seedy elegance.

As a child, Pryor spent many an evening sitting on the veranda swing and dreaming of what lay beyond the hill opposite. She loved to hear the train whistle in the night. It seemed to announce the existence of places like Paris, London and Cairo.

It had been a limited life, her living with the two aging aunts and her despondent mother. More and more her mother talked of beautiful Charleston—the balls, garden parties and teas. She'd loved her Russian husband, mourned his death for years. But as time passed she grew increasingly homesick.

There was little social life in Overton. It was dirt poor. The vein of coal had run out. The miners went into farming or left. Those in management mostly had moved to Pittsburgh. All activity centered on the main street which boasted the Bison Theatre, a small department store, a hardware store that also offered shoe repairs, a grocery story, a drugstore, and other tiny assorted shops.

Pryor loved the Bison Theatre. Each Saturday night the aunts took her there, after which they'd have a soda at the drugstore.

She was educated by the Sisters of St. Francis in a girls-only school on a hill beyond the main street. Pryor enjoyed the school and the nuns. They were gentle, kind women, eager to introduce her to the *Idylls of the King*, to explain the reproductions on the walls of paintings by Cimabue, Giotto and Raphael. Pryor had one close friend, Evelyn. Evelyn was tall, spindly, with frizzy brown hair and horned-rimmed glasses.

Pryor was neither brilliant nor stupid. She was a favorite of the nuns. There were no boys to worry about. She was not a Catholic and the nuns didn't try to convert her.

When she graduated, she went to work in Overton's only bookstore. There were not many customers, so she could read to her heart's content. The insurance money from the fire which took Bella, Katia, and her mother enabled her to rent a tiny apartment on the top floor of Mildred Arquette's house, another Victorian ruin. She played bridge on Thursday nights with a group assembled by her friend Evelyn. She went to the Methodist church every Sunday and to the young people's gathering at the church on Sunday nights.

It was at the bookstore that she met Harold McNulty, whose Viking good looks matched the heroes of both nineteenth-century novels and cheaper current romances. Pryor bought two new dresses, some modestly priced cologne, and even applied lipstick, but he had eyes only for the blond, lisping proprietress, Bebe.

She went to two young people's dances at the church, dragged by Evelyn. She was asked to dance twice, once by George Harmon, druggist, widower, and at least forty-eight. He was overweight, almost bald, and needed new glasses. She next danced with Homer Frye, who smelled of sauerkraut and whose mouth was permanently agape. After Homer she fled home and vowed to avoid any more social occasions.

It was a couple of sterile years before she met Mark Whiteside. He came into the bookstore, looking for Walker Percy's *Love in the Ruins*, which amazingly was available. As Percy was a favorite author of Pryor's, they couldn't help getting into a conversation.

Mark Whiteside was not as drop-dead handsome as Harold McNulty, but he was tall, well built, and had a thin, intellectual face. His voice was deep, educated, soft, and he seemed a bit shy. It took three more visits to the shop before he ventured to ask Pryor out to dinner. ''I'm new in town,'' he said, ''and don't make friends easily. Besides, you can give me more information about our enigmatic Walker Percy.''

She changed her dress three times getting ready for her date, but she assured herself that this was of no importance, a chance encounter and no more.

His car, like his clothes, was elegant but not new, a Ferrari, he told her when she asked. They drove about three miles along the river and then cut back into the hills. When they stopped it was at a low-slung building made chiefly of fieldstone. But the inside had its own rural charm, with heart pine floors, shelves of well-read books, an inconspicuous fire on the hearth.

Pryor found it all dreamlike.

They talked of Percy's books while eating a spectacular dinner. Pryor wished that she'd worn something more dazzling than a navy dress with white collar and cuffs. But Mark made her feel attractive and intelligent, someone special.

''Tell me about your Russian relatives,'' he said suddenly.

Pryor looked at him in amazement. ''How did you know?''

''Your name, those high, wide cheekbones

and slightly slanted eyes. On the other hand, you could have sat for Botticelli.''

Over dessert, she explained about her musician father, Charleston mother, and two old aunts.

When she told him about the fire, his face was filled with compassion.

''You poor little lamb, to be thrust out on your own so young. To be doomed to live in that dreary town.''

It turned out that Mark had an aunt who lived in that dreary town, in one of those big houses. When her husband, a coal magnate, died, she stayed on and became something of a recluse. When Mark came to Overton he stayed with her.

Pryor couldn't believe how at ease she felt with him. Up to then most of what she knew of men came from Evelyn, a born cynic. Men were a breed apart, not to be trusted. ''They're only after one thing,'' Evelyn had told her ominously. It seemed Mark Whiteside was the exception. He occasionally touched her hand and his eyes enveloped her, but he always was a gentleman. He took her to lunch, to dinner, to walks in the hills, to ballets and symphony concerts in Pittsburgh. He quoted Shakespeare and Shelley.

She never met his aunt. "When the time is right," he assured her, "I'll take you by for a visit." That time never came.

She mentioned Mark only to Evelyn, who, as usual, was the cynic but nevertheless intrigued. "But what does he do?" she pressed.

The next time they were together Pryor asked him. She'd wanted to ask before but he seemed reluctant to talk about himself.

It was several seconds before he answered her with a smile. "I'm what you might call 'independently wealthy.' It leaves me free to do what I love most. Write poetry. Paint a little. I had a book of poems published a few years ago."

She vowed silently to look for it in the library. She glanced at him with shining eyes. He was quite perfect, the essence of romance. At that moment she was close to loving him.

Pryor would lie in bed at night and wonder what it would be like to be held in Mark's arms, to be kissed by him. She found out.

They'd been walking in the woods of chestnut trees and maples on an especially hot day when they came to a satin-smooth pond. At one end were water lilies. Pryor was enchanted. "I know," said Mark suddenly, "I'll go for a swim."

Suddenly he was pulling off his clothes, the white pants and blue shirt, revealing blue-and-white swim trunks. Then he dove into the pond, a graceful, clean dive. She stood motionless, watching him. He swam for several minutes, then looking back at her, grabbed a water lily and waded ashore. He stood before her, as perfect as a Greek statue. He tangled the water lily in her hair.

His eyes moved from her narrow hips and much narrower waist to her face. He moved closer, pressed her against him. She could feel the smooth power of his muscles.

When his lips touched hers she was transformed, another person in another land. He kissed her neck and shoulders. She was aware only of him.

Then he pulled away from her abruptly. He said nothing. She watched him put on his clothes, and there was no conversation as they walked back to the car. They didn't speak as he drove them to Overton. Pryor told herself that words would confuse them both just then. They didn't speak when he pulled up at her door, and she got out of the car and went in the house.

She sat in a rocking chair by the window and watched the sunset over the river, the first stars appear. She still was exhilarated, amazed at the capacity to care she'd found in herself. She was a whole woman, now that this man cared for her. She'd been reinvented. She longed to have Mark beside her now, to feel the gentleness of his hands, the touch of his lips. Still longing, she finally fell asleep.

She waited for his call or for him to come into the bookshop. She waited in vain, a day, a week, a month. Maybe something had happened to him. There was no one to let her know. She finally decided that he'd found her somehow lacking and was avoiding a commitment. When she at last decided to call him on the pretext of another Percy book, she realized she had neither his phone number nor address. In the Overton phone book there was no listing of a Whiteside, male or female.

Somehow she got through the days, the endless nights. It was Evelyn who brought things to a head. "Okay, pal," she said, "Let's have it. What did I do to offend?" Pryor stared at her as they stood on a street corner in the rain. "You can't be spending every minute with Mark Whiteside," Evelyn accused.

Suddenly she had to tell someone about it and she knew Evelyn was the one. They went into Daisy's Café, ordered coffee, and looked warily at each other. Pryor was appalled to find she was crying. Then she was telling Evelyn everything.

"And you haven't heard from him since?" Evelyn was cleaning her glasses with a paper napkin.

"No. It's been almost two months. He has a mother and father living in Pittsburgh. In a suburb called Fox Chapel."

"Big bucks, you can bet. Did you call him there?"

"Yes. They said he was out of the country."

Evelyn didn't berate her or even comment on Pryor's account. She finished her coffee and pushed back her chair.

"I know a cop on the Pittsburgh police force. He owes me one. I'd like to ask him to find out what he can about your Mark. Okay?"

"Okay," said Pryor weakly.

For two days and nights she barely slept, barely ate. She felt like a crazy woman. It was nothing compared to the way she felt when Evelyn called with her news. Mark Whiteside was the son of a prestigious Pittsburgh family. He'd attended a New England private school and completed one year at Princeton. In the following ten years, he'd been incarcerated in three different psychiatric hospitals, diagnosed

as having a severe psychosis with manic de-
pressive tendencies.

In the mail, that very day, Pryor received an
official-looking letter from Charleston. It was
from a lawyer and informed her that she'd been
named in her Aunt Althea's will. It requested
that she appear in Charleston three days hence.
Enclosed was the money for airline tickets and
an assurance that the proper accommodations
would be provided, including someone to meet
her plane.

Pryor and Evelyn mulled over the letter for
some time.

"Don't get your hopes up," said the ever-
cynical Evelyn. "Your Aunt Althea's probably
left you an ugly garnet brooch."

"Charleston," murmured Pryor, almost cra-
dling the word.

"Or," Evelyn went on, "an even uglier
locket with a tress of your great-grandmother's
hair." She paused, looked at Pryor closely.
"Don't tell me. You're going, aren't you?"

Chapter Three

Pryor was awakened by something touching her face. She opened her eyes. A Siamese cat was calmly licking her chin. She sat up, looked around. She was in the canopied bed, wearing a delicate batiste nightgown. Across the bottom of the bed lay a rose satin robe. She realized that she had passed out the night before. Exhaustion, stress, and shock had been too much for her.

The cat leaped onto a chair and from the back of the chair onto the mantel. Maneuvering past the decorative paperweights, it lay down, staring at her with defiance.

Egypt and Sylvia must have put her to bed.

Her suitcase, unopened, sat by the chaise longue. Three million dollars. She couldn't comprehend it. She could think only of the years she'd lived in a drab apartment, eking out the fire insurance money, carefully invested. She thought of her job as cashier in a bookstore, the endless tunafish sandwiches, the clothes always bought on sale.

She was about to get up but a tap on the door stopped her. "Come in," she half whispered. Sylvia, bearing a silver tray, entered.

"Brought you some breakfast." She glanced at the cat on the mantel. "That's Persis. She must like you." She settled the tray on Pryor's knees and beamed at her.

Pryor stared down at orange juice, eggs and bacon, English muffin, butter, jelly, and a small pot of coffee. "Thank you."

Sylvia stood with the air of someone waiting. Finally she spoke. "You want I should get out your clothes? I always got out Miss Althea's."

"Thank you."

"Somethin' else."

"Yes?"

"You want I should stay on?"

Pryor looked carefully at the woman. Despite the lack of wrinkles, she saw someone a little beyond her prime. ''Isn't this big house a lot to take care of?''

Sylvia's expression was a combination of scorn and pity. ''There's Helen, the cleaning woman; Hermine, the laundress, and Jacob, the handyman and gardener.''

''I see.'' Pryor thought of the three million. ''Would you ask them to stay on for a while?''

''Yes'm.''

Sylvia disappeared into the closet, ignoring the suitcase. Pryor proceeded to eat her breakfast. She was on the second English muffin when Sylvia reappeared bearing a lightweight wool dress, pale lilac and full skirted, and a pair of high-heeled tan pumps.

Pryor regarded these with consternation. ''I have my own clothes. I—''

''Miz Althea bought you these, the whole closet. She went all the way to Atlanta.''

Pryor suddenly realized that her aunt intended her to dress for her new position as a Charleston heiress. ''Thank you, Sylvia,'' she murmured.

Sylvia disappeared with the tray. Pryor showered and dressed, then slipped on the lilac dress and shoes and stood before the pier glass in wonderment. Persis had jumped from the mantel and rubbed against her legs. It was not the same person who had sat on the plane in the stained polyester suit. She added a string of pearls, a high school graduation present from her mother and aunts. Her hair held its pageboy cut. She applied lipstick, realizing that her wide-set blue eyes needed no makeup.

She tried to revel in her new appearance, but something Egypt had said suddenly intruded. She'd paid no attention to Egypt's announcement the day before, but now it rang in her memory. Egypt had been speaking of the missing Rose.

"It's my opinion that she's dead. And not by natural causes."

Egypt believed that Rose, Althea's young daughter, either was a suicide or was murdered.

It was all beyond Pryor's comprehension— the money, the house, and now Egypt's incredible accusation.

She had a second cup of coffee in the downstairs drawing room. It was exquisitely proportioned with Adam woodwork and furniture that glowed with age and care. Pryor sat on a Sheraton sofa, gazing at the mirror above the fireplace, the silk curtains, Aubusson rug.

Sylvia paged her for two telephone calls. One was Miranda asking if she and Linda could stop by later in the day; the other was Winthrop

Hazzard, asking if he could take her to dinner that night. To each she responded with a muted ''yes.''

She returned to the sofa, sat quietly, trying to regain a sense of order. She hadn't planned on staying in Charleston. She'd supposed that her aunt had left her a modest sum or a piece of family jewelry. Instead she'd been thrust into a new life, a new identity. The thought of Rose kept intruding. Apparently Althea, too, thought Rose was dead. She'd not mentioned her in the will. Pryor shivered. The sun had vanished and the room suddenly was darker.

She went back upstairs, pausing on the landing, where an oriel window looked into the garden next door. She saw the holes in the ground first, then the old man who was digging them. He was conversing with a young man who, stretched on a lounge chair, was drinking from a wineglass. The bottle was on the table beside him. The young man, darkly tanned, wore only faded shorts, was barefoot, and looked like an Olympic athlete. Tall and muscular, he had brown-black curly hair and a rugged face. Suddenly he put down his glass, rose, and took the old man's shovel. He dug slowly, carefully, and finally leaned down and drew something from the hole. It was a dish with a small bit missing.

He handed it to the old man, who cheered, turned to the table, and poured wine into two glasses. They toasted, lifting their glasses and laughing with pleasure.

"The peculiar Perrigeaus," said a voice behind her. She turned to find Egypt, beautifully dressed in a gray suit, smiling broadly. "The old one is Bubber. His life work is digging up aged artifacts in his garden. The young one is Thomas, his nephew."

"Whose life work is sitting in the garden at ten in the morning, drinking wine."

"Not exactly. Thomas is a journalist. International. Also an author. He's written two books about the frays he's covered."

"How do you know so much, Egypt?"

"I'm curious and I'm nosy. Come on, I'll show you around."

There were four bedrooms on the second floor. The two guest rooms were simply but impeccably furnished. Althea's room was another matter. It was cluttered. There was a massive four-poster bed with at least a dozen small lacy pillows, silver-framed photographs on every flat surface, chairs with petit-point seats and matching stools. On one wall hung a big portrait, a golden-haired beauty sitting on a low wall. She wore a filmy dress. There were diamonds around her neck and one wrist, diamonds on several fingers. An odd-looking watch stood out.

Pryor pointed to it. ''What's that? It doesn't quite fit.''

Egypt laughed. ''Of course not. It's a Mickey Mouse watch. Rose wore it because the contrast with all those diamonds amused her. It amused Althea as well, drove Miranda crazy. Rose was born wild, antic. In staid proper Charleston, she was her mother's secret entertainment.''

Egypt identified the photographs, introducing her to some of her forebears, then she took Pryor by the arm. ''Come on. I'll show you the garden.''

They went downstairs and out one of the drawing room French doors onto a seventy-foot piazza with a white rail and tall white pillars. An old black man with a rake waved to them from the far end of the garden. He was cleaning the pool that surrounded a statue of a cherub.

By Pryor's standards, it was mild for October, not at all like Pennsylvania. She listened to Egypt pointing out what grew in each flower bed, also indicating wisteria, magnolia, crepe myrtle, and plane trees. She observed an obviously empty spot by the steps leading down from the piazza. ''There was a gorgeous magnolia there, but Hurricane Hugo got it. Althea was inconsolable, could never bring herself to replace it. Now you can decide.''

When Pryor told Egypt about the upcoming visit of Miranda and Linda, Egypt sighed. ''I wonder what tack they will take, whether they will let bygones be bygones or eradicate you with the famous Charleston chill.''

''Maybe they want to be friendly. After all, we *are* kin.''

''How new-hatched you are!'' She squeezed Pryor's arm. ''Don't listen to me. I'm just an unreconstructed old cynic.''

''Are you married, Egypt?''

''No. But almost. It took me years to find a significant other in my league.''

Egypt went off to a business appointment. Pryor unpacked her suitcase, brooded over the clothing she'd folded with such consternation and hope back in Overton. It all looked like something out of a mission barrel. She kept her bits of inexpensive jewelry and decided to give the rest to Goodwill.

She had lunch alone in the spacious dining room, eating a delicious lobster salad at the polished Queen Anne table. Sylvia asked if she'd like wine but she declined. She called Goodwill, then asked Sylvia to put her old suitcase of clothes on the piazza where it could be picked up. She called her astonished landlady in Overton, saying she wouldn't be returning, then called the bookstore where she'd worked and resigned. She thought of phoning a few friends but decided to write to them instead.

Promptly at four o'clock Miranda and Linda arrived. Miranda, wearing a simple but expensive-looking skirt and blouse, made Pryor feel overdressed. Her tawny hair was pulled into a French twist; her heavily lashed green eyes were neutral. Linda, whose dull blond-brown hair was parted in the middle and clung in tight curls below her ears, had disguised a slightly overweight figure with a narrow skirt and long overblouse. She followed her sister, who sailed into the drawing room and planted herself on the pale striped sofa. Pryor stood uneasily, then pulled up a chair.

"Well," Miranda spoke as if opening a meeting, "our reason for coming by is to see if we can be of any use."

Pryor looked helplessly into the green eyes which, suddenly, were friendly. "That's very kind of you," she said.

"Not at all."

They discussed Charleston weather, the people who would be coming to call.

"Abigail Browning out of curiosity," announced Miranda. "Cynthia Talbot out of a sense of duty."

There were numerous, if tactful, questions about Pryor's history. She told them about her Russian father, who died young; about her and her mother living with Bella and Katia; the fire; her job at the bookstore.

Miranda was guarded in her response. Linda clucked with pity.

"Doubtless you're undergoing quite a culture shock," observed Miranda.

"Yes, I am. Look"—Pryor leaned forward— "I feel badly. The inheritance should have gone to you two. I didn't even know your mother."

"She was rash and unpredictable. She always felt that I was a bit dull, and Linda, here, hopelessly plain."

Linda blushed, sneezed, groped in her purse for a handkerchief.

"I have twin boys," said Miranda, "who will be going to college next year, a heavily mortgaged house, and a husband who has suffered severe losses in the stock market. Linda,"—she nodded toward her sister—"is not in much better shape." Her face sagged. "Mother knew all that."

Pryor had never felt more uncomfortable. "I'm sorry."

"I'm sure you are."

"Did you ever go ice-skating?" Linda's non sequitur was sudden, out of the blue.

Pryor stared at her. Miranda glared at her. "Yes, I have."

"I've heard that you have hard freezes in Pennsylvania, big snows."

"We do." Pryor realized that Linda was clumsily trying to cover for her sister's obvious play for pity. She realized also that Miranda hoped to get her hands on some of the three million.

It was an opportune moment for Sylvia's arrival with a big silver tray. Pryor poured carefully from the silver teapot, passed the watercress sandwiches and petit fours. She wondered if her cousins had been letting bygones be bygones or giving her the Charleston chill. She noticed that the teacups were as thin as eggshells and her hands shook a little.

It wasn't until they were leaving that Pryor sensed warmth. Miranda put an arm around her. "I hope you'll come to dinner with Bruce and me real soon," she said. "We'd like to know you better. After all, you are our cousin."

"I will. That would be fun."

"Miranda," said Linda, "has a wonderful cook."

Pryor watched them go out by the big front door, down the marble steps to a waiting Cadillac convertible.

Later she put her cousins out of her mind and, watched by Persis, lolled in a huge tub, enjoying the perfume and bubbles of bath oil. She still was grasping for the lay of the land, what she would do with her newfound wealth. She reviewed the things she always had wanted. They were few—a cashmere sweater, about ten books, a trip to Europe. All were within her grasp. She let herself think about Winthrop Hazzard, decided he was not within her grasp. Oddly enough, she thought instead of Harold McNulty back in Overton. He'd hardly noticed her, overlooked her admiring glances, concentrating on Bebe Nelson, who owned the bookstore. Bebe was blond, sexy, lisped, and read very few of the books that lined her shelves. Pryor wondered what Harold would think if she reappeared in Overton, sporting her Mercedes, a mink coat, and a gold cigarette holder.

At a few minutes after seven, wearing a svelte black taffeta dress, black high-heeled sandals, and her pearls, she opened the door to Winthrop Hazzard.

She enjoyed seeing his eyes widen with appreciation as he helped her into a fur stole. He led her to a dark blue Jaguar.

He didn't say where they were going. He didn't say much of anything. He smelled faintly of eucalyptus. He drew up in front of a marquee with the name MICHELLE'S on it, and ushered her out of the car. Inside was a dim, attractive room with a bar on one side and portraits adorning the brick walls. They were greeted by a smiling young man, who led them to a table in an adjoining room. Once the young man had taken their order—mussels in wine sauce, filet Bordelaise with a St. Estephe claret, a salad— Winthrop Hazzard leaned forward. He inspected her as if viewing a previously undiscovered art treasure. She wondered why he hadn't consulted her about the menu, and decided it was the way men of the world did things.

His eloquent gray eyes were openly admiring but not speculative.

''I know this is a social occasion and not a business dinner,'' said Pryor, ''but I must ask if you plan to stay on as lawyer for the estate.''

''I will be glad to.''

''You've been my aunt's lawyer for ten

years, and I see no reason to make a change. That is, I trust Aunt Althea's judgment.''

His face relaxed. He smiled. ''Her investments were handled by Forest, Gray, and Winter. A great deal of her income was reinvested. She drew about five thousand a month.''

Pryor wondered what she would do with five thousand, then thought of the huge house, the servants, utilities, taxes.

''That's fine with me,'' she said weakly.

''Good. Now we can talk about more important things, like you.''

''Me?''

''Your likes and dislikes, impressions of Charleston, hopes for the future.''

In essence, she told him what she had revealed to Miranda and Linda. Then she dared a question. ''Now it's your turn.''

He told her about growing up in an old Philadelphia family, the loss of his parents, going to Harvard Law School, deciding to come to Charleston.

''Why Charleston?'' she asked.

''My grandmother was a Charlestonian. I used to visit here. I spent many summers at her beach house. I don't know—'' He toyed with a spoon. ''It always was a special place for me, beautiful, orderly, and distanced from the rat race.'' His face suddenly looked sad, vulnerable. ''We all have to find a place where we can survive.''

''Have you a family here?'' She held her breath.

''If you mean wife and kiddies, no.''

She was surprised but delighted.

He laughed, a deep, beguiling laugh. ''Charlestonians generally marry each other.''

''You never were tempted?''

He leaned back, still smiling. ''Oh, of course. There was Mary Ellen Clark, but she was a giggler. Sue Beth Anderson never stopped talking. Alice Gibson was given to causes, was always carrying candles for this or that group in Marion Square.''

She knew he was teasing her but she didn't care. ''Tell me about Rose.''

It was several seconds before he answered. ''Rosie was one of a kind. Full of life, unsuited to Charleston. She and Althea were very close.''

''But the will—''

''Althea knew that Rosie simply wouldn't disappear. She had detectives on her trail for years. Nothing. One night Rosie left the house and has been gone for years.''

''What do you think, Mr. Hazzard?''

"Win, please. I don't know what I think. Nor does anyone else. Althea kept hoping she'd show up. By the time she wrote that will she'd accepted that Rose was gone for good."

"How terribly sad."

"Yes."

All at once, Pryor was exhausted. It had been a long, eventful day. She knew Win would understand that. "This has been a lovely dinner," she said, "but I'm really pretty tired."

"Of course." He called for the bill. In minutes they were back in the Jaguar, heading for Tradd Street.

Pryor admitted to herself that it had not been a romantic evening. But at the door, Win gave her a long look, took her hand, and very gently kissed it.

Chapter Four

The next morning she lay in bed and thought about the dinner at Michelle's, the kiss on her hand. In the cold light of day it seemed to have happened to a different person. But then she *was* a different person. She gazed at the cat Persis who curled beside her, at the utterly feminine room. How long would it take her to feel at home here? She reflected that she'd never felt at home anywhere, not in the hotel rooms with her parents, not in Bella and Katia's house, not in her dreary apartment. At times she felt disoriented, like a creature from unknown parts. One friend had called her disengaged, another accused her of being only half present.

41

She rose, walked across the room, and looked in the pier glass. There was the same face, wide-spaced blue eyes, small straight nose, well-shaped mouth. It should have been a pretty face but she concluded that it wasn't. Her red-blond hair waved to her shoulders; her figure was slim but not sensational. She stood on long slender legs. There were no bad points, but the whole added up to plainness.

She wondered how Win Hazzard saw her, if his admiring glance was one of mere kindness or cordiality.

"Ready for some breakfast?" Sylvia spoke from the doorway, tray in hand.

Pryor went back to her bed and ate her breakfast while Sylvia stood eyeing her. "You have a good time last night?" she finally asked.

Pryor gave Persis a bite of bacon. "Yes."

"Mr. Win, he's a nice man. So special lookin'. You can't go wrong with Mr. Win. He's a gentleman."

"I guess so."

"You can be sure he's not after your money. Got plenty of his own."

"That's nice."

Sylvia went to the closet and brought back a pair of designer jeans, a blue silk shirt, and flat sandals. "You're not goin' out, are you?"

"No."

"Then these here will do."

Egypt appeared at about eleven o'clock, looking like a fashion plate in a red wool dress. "I've got some papers from the Hazzard office for you to sign." Pryor sat at the dining room table and signed them.

"You didn't read them," Egypt objected.

"I trust you. Besides, I'm sure you've read them."

Egypt laughed. "You're right." She gathered up the papers, put them in her briefcase, and went to the kitchen to greet her mother.

Pryor wandered out to the garden, a haven of greenness, the well-clipped lawn with its neat flower beds stretching back to the pond. She didn't see Jacob, decided he didn't work that day, but she did see a tall, shirtless figure coming through the gate. Thomas Perrigeau. His smile seemed to encompass the world.

"You're Pryor Dimitri?"

"Yes."

"Thomas Perrigeau here. Will you marry me?"

"No."

"I was afraid of that. I've been looking all over for an heiress. None would have me."

Pryor put her hands in her pockets and stared at him. "What are your qualifications?"

"I was an Eagle Scout. Upright, forthright, and so forth. I'm honest, kind to children and animals, can cook, garden, and I don't snore."

"A dazzling résumé."

"You're prettier than I expected. Nothing sly or hidden in that face. Have you ever been in love?"

"No."

"Would you give it a try?"

"No."

"A lady in flight. Distrustful not only of the world but herself as well."

"Really?"

"If you won't accept my proposal, perhaps you'll accept a modest gift."

"A gift?" He was making her nervous.

"Something I'd promised Althea—a magnolia tree for that empty spot near the piazza. We both agreed it would be perfect."

"That's kind of you."

"I have to fly to the Midwest tomorrow on an assignment, but as soon as I get back I'll plant it."

She wished he'd go. Her reactions to this man were not within her frame of reference. She stared at his bronze chest, arms, and legs,

then looked elsewhere. ''That will be fine.''
She edged away.

''In the meantime, you might consider my abrupt but heartfelt proposal. Winsome Win is really not for you.'' She watched him go back out the gate and disappear.

''Phone for you,'' said Sylvia from the doorway.

It was Winthrop Hazzard, asking if she'd be free to join him for lunch at the beach on Sunday. She begged off, not knowing why, annoyed with herself.

She sat in the library, going over the household accounts with Sylvia. She kept toying with her new checkbook, left for her by Win. Besides the five thousand, he'd left a savings account at her disposal.

''The keys for the car,'' said Sylvia, handing them to her. ''Egypt left them. Lamb chops okay for dinner?''

''Yes, thank you.''

Sylvia went to the door, turned, came back. She spoke softly. ''Pryor, don't worry. You'll feel good pretty soon. Takes time.''

''It does indeed.'' Egypt was in the room, beaming. She sat near Pryor, crossed her spectacular legs. ''I came to give you a few pointers on living in Charleston.''

At seeing Pryor's expression, she spoke quickly. "Oh, it's not in my realm, but Althea often confided in me. We giggled about it together."

"I can use all the help I can get."

"That's my girl. First, don't give any big parties for the first six months. You'll be invited out, but they'll only be sizing you up. Two, never mention money, never drop names. Be frank about your forebears. Thank heaven, you came from Pennsylvania."

"Why?"

"It's accepted to be from away, beyond the pale to be from upstate."

"How silly."

"Of course. Manners are important here. Values, also. If you're new it helps to be interesting. In Charleston if you have good manners and something to offer, half the battle is won."

"I have little to offer. What's the other half?"

"What I've told you will do for starters. I've got to go." She rose, picked up her purse. At the door she turned. "One more thing—don't ever cry at funerals or weddings. The locals conceal their emotions, never display them." With this she was gone.

There were a lot of things Pryor wanted to

ask her but they would have to wait. She wished she had asked about Thomas Perrigeau.

She went back upstairs to her room. Persis followed. She glanced at the canopied bed, chaise longue, and dressing table, and something occurred to her. This had been Rose's room. She felt it in her bones. This was where Rose had slept, dreamed her dreams, packed a bag for each of her trips. She saw none of Rose's intimate possessions, but an aura remained. Her own things filled the drawers of the bureau and closet.

She went to the desk, sat on a delicate chair, and pulled open the drawer. Nothing. Nothing but a scratch pad. She had hoped for a diary maybe. The scratch pad was full of numbers, additions and subtractions. She put it back, closed the drawer.

She thought the beach might be interesting in October, and wished she had accepted Win's invitation. It still was warm during the day. They might have walked on the sand. They might have . . . She knew why she had refused him. She was never one to have impossible expectations.

Egypt had been right about the invitations. They poured in, some written, others delivered by phone. Wearing her beautiful new clothes, she went to luncheons, dinner parties, cocktail parties. She found the Charlestonians charming, if a little aloof. She never mentioned money or dropped names. She found that the men did most of the talking and she could get away with an occasional "Is that so?" or "I declare."

She felt pleased with her ability to adapt. Egypt, who gleaned information from various servants, reported that there were no adverse reviews. In an odd way she was beginning to feel at home, as if she belonged. She considered this sensation with her usual wariness.

She called a few friends in Overton and explained what had befallen her, suffered through their exclamations of astonishment and envy. She wrote thank-you notes for the parties she'd attended, read Althea's collection of nineteenth-century female authors. Often she stood in her closet and looked at the collection of clothing, all silk, cotton, or wool. In a bureau drawer she found six cashmere sweaters. She went to the bank, opened Althea's strongbox, and surveyed the jewelry now in her name. It was not a dazzling collection but it was all real—several lengths of pearls, some dinner rings, jade bracelets, brooches. She remembered the portrait of Rose, the diamond necklace and bracelet. She wondered if Althea had given equivalent jewelry to Miranda and Linda. She hoped so.

She had Jacob plant a fig tree in the empty spot by the piazza. A few days later she and Jacob stood looking at the dead twigs.

"Done all I should," said Jacob. "Musta been a sad li'l tree to begin with. I'll dig it up. We'll plant somethin' else."

"No." Thomas Perrigeau had been gone for about a week. He must be back by now. She wanted him to see that she'd made an effort on her own. She would not take orders from him.

But when he phoned that afternoon, asking her to dinner the following night, she heard herself accepting.

"Don't dress up," he said. "I'm not taking you to a posh French restaurant."

He didn't. He took her to a modest seafood place out near the beach. It was a warm night and they sat on a terrace looking over a small inlet and expanse of marsh. Her exquisitely cut ecru silk suit was perfect. Thomas wore a navy blazer, shirt, tie, and lightweight gray pants. His curly, dark hair was carefully combed.

He seemed more civilized, less antic. After they'd finished their poached salmon and sautéed shrimp and discussed a few Charleston oddities, especially his Uncle Bubber, she dared ask about Rose.

Thomas, like Win Hazzard, didn't answer at once. He looked out over the marsh, observed the three-quarter moon.

"I think she's dead."

"Why?"

"She wouldn't have stayed away from home this long. She would have come back to Althea or at least called. Rose was a bit of a card, but she was consistent in important things."

"How was she a card?"

"Tying ripe apples on her grandmother's pear tree at night in the dead of winter; skinny-dipping in the park fountain."

"Were you in love with her?"

"No, but I admired her." Thomas loosened his tie. His expression became less serious. "I hope it matters to you."

"No. I'm just curious."

"What would you do if I were to grab you in a wild embrace, force passionate kisses upon you?"

Once more she could see the antic delight in his eyes, the wide smile.

"I'd fight back or jump in the water."

She'd learned no more about Rose, little about Thomas. There was no wild embrace.

They finished their dinner and drove back to town in Thomas's rather battered van.

At her door, there were no passionate kisses. He simply stood for a moment, looking deeply into her eyes. "Take care," he said.

She didn't go to sleep for a long time. She lay in bed, Persis at her side, looking at the shaft of moonlight drifting into her room. She wondered why Thomas had told her to take care. The old house suddenly seemed threatening. Her Aunt Bella would have said it had bad vibes, no residue of happiness. Certainly Althea had found no happiness in her daughters, except for Rose. Then Rose disappeared. She decided that she, Pryor Dimitri, had become Althea's project. Althea had discovered that her sister's daughter had been living in semi-poverty with few prospects for anything different. She'd decided to change all that. Pryor thought of Aunt Althea's pleasure in buying the perfect clothes in the perfect size, changing her will, envisioning the future consternation of Miranda and Linda.

She decided that she'd been used to further Althea's revenge on her daughters and life itself. She tried to be angry about this. Before she managed, she was asleep.

Chapter Five

The next morning she made what seemed a momentous decision. She invited Miranda and Bruce Garner, Linda and Cleve Martin, and Win Hazzard to dinner. All of them accepted. She immediately regretted this. They all, except Win, resented, even hated her.

On the chosen day, the house glowed with polished furniture, glittering chandeliers, and vases of fall flowers in hallway, drawing and dining room. Sylvia had found a female cousin to help her with the serving. Pryor selected a glamorous outfit from her closet, flowing green chiffon pants and an overblouse with small jeweled buttons. Sylvia, aided by Egypt, had

52

planned a tasty meal of crabmeat cocktail, veal Marsala, herbed rice, and asparagus vinaigrette. For dessert there was a fruit compote.

They all were close to half an hour late. Pryor was not surprised. Egypt has warned her that Charlestonians always were at least twenty minutes late. Anything earlier was considered déclassé. The women wore beautiful pantsuits, Miranda's white wool and Linda's black velvet. The men in their impeccable suits turned the beflowered drawing room into a page from *Town & Country.*

Win poured the drinks at a side table. They chatted amiably. They laughed. The good humor continued in the dining room. The sly look had left Miranda's face. She eyed the perfect table, even Pryor, with warmth and pleasure. Linda beamed. They all had second helpings. Rose was mentioned only once during dinner. It was Linda who looked around the table and made the observation. ''We look like a real family, except for Mother, and of course Rosie.''

There was a moment of silence and then Pryor spoke. ''One thing I'm going to do with Aunt Althea's money is find out what happened to Rose. I've only got a few leads but I promise you I'll find out.''

Back in the drawing room, the joviality returned. Bruce Garner, Miranda's husband, and Cleve Martin, Linda's, couldn't have been more engaging. Pryor liked the way Bruce leaned forward, arms on his knees, when he was asking about her likes and dislikes. She was beguiled by the handsome Cleve's look of sophistication and final display of naïveté. Win Hazzard was charm itself, regaling them with jokes and surprising them with his recall of the lyrics of old Cole Porter and George Gershwin tunes.

Aided by more drinks, they sang without accompaniment. Miranda, an acceptable contralto, contributed "Someone to Watch Over Me." Bruce, a chancy tenor, tried "Stout-Hearted Men;" Cleve rather shyly opted for "Bye, Bye Blackbird," and Linda, after considerable urging, launched into "Over the Rainbow." When they all looked at Pryor, she, bolstered by years in the church choir in Overton, sang "Moon River." It was Win who surprised them by singing and relishing all the verses of "Kitty from Kansas City."

Pryor couldn't have been more pleased with herself. They were like a gathering of old friends or a family reunion. She'd seldom felt part of a group before. She actually was sorry when the evening was over and they filed out the front door with promises of get-togethers soon, brief hugs and smiles. Win was the last, his hug and smile less brief.

Pryor insisted on helping with the cleanup of drawing and dining room. She and Sylvia basked in their success.

''You're a real good hostess, missy. Like you were born to it.''

''Thank you, Sylvia. The meal was a triumph.''

''Miz Althea would be real proud of you.''

''I hope so.''

It wasn't until she was climbing the long stairway that she realized how tired she was. It hadn't been an ordeal, but it demanded every ounce of her concentration and joie de vivre.

Persis already was stretched out on Pryor's bed, lifting her head for a bare second, then settling back. Pryor was grateful for the cat, feeling as usual a twinge of trepidation at staying alone in the big house.

She washed her face, brushed her teeth, slipped on a pale pink voile nightgown, and crawled into bed, Persis beside her. For the first time she felt that the house belonged to her. The beautiful Spode china and George II flatware were hers. What had seemed beyond belief to her was slowly being taken for granted.

She reviewed the evening, particularly Win Hazzard's contribution—his charm, sense of humor, eloquent good looks. She decided that their friendship never would go beyond that, but she knew she could depend on him and was grateful. Miranda and Linda held the promise of friendship as well. So did Bruce and Cleve. She smiled, thinking that the trip she hadn't wanted to make had brought her not only a fortune, but a wonderful sense of family.

Exhausted, lulled by the cool October breeze coming through the French doors, she slept at last.

When she first heard the sound, she ignored it, looked at her bedside clock, and decided it must be coming from next door. No one would call on her in the middle of the night. It came again, a sharp knocking. Persis raised her head and jumped to the floor. By that time Pryor knew the sound was the front door knocker. Someone must be in trouble, must need her. Egypt or Sylvia, maybe, or a tourist in desperation. She swung her legs over the side of the bed and slipped on rose satin slippers and the matching robe.

With Persis walking regally ahead of her, she stepped into the upstairs hall which was seldom lit. The only light came from the telephone table downstairs. Persis started down the steps, Pryor following.

''I'm coming,'' she shouted, but the knock grew louder.

She almost tripped over the cat. Persis had stopped cold and was sniffing at something just ahead of her. She lifted a paw and touched what was invisible to Pryor. As soon as Pryor leaned forward and knelt on the step above Persis, she saw what the cat saw. A length of nylon cord stretched across the step ahead, secured to a bannister and, with a small nail, attached to the wall.

Pryor sat on a step above trying to take in what the cat had discovered. Persis crawled under the cord and continued downstairs. The knocking had stopped. A deep shuddering seemed to take control of Pryor's body. Arms around her knees, she closed her eyes, trying to will away the horror. Someone had planned that she'd go down the steps to answer the door, trip over the cord, and fall headlong to the bottom. Someone was trying to hurt her badly or have her end in death.

She sat for several minutes then rose slowly, stepped over the cord, and proceeded down the steps. Who wanted to hurt her badly? Who wouldn't have minded if she was dead? She stopped by the phone, stared at it. She'd recovered enough to know she needed help. Egypt's number was not hard to find. She dialed, waited numbly. Egypt's voice sounded distant, sleepy. "Yes."

"Egypt, it's Pryor. I need you. Can you come?"

Egypt didn't ask why. She spoke quickly, calmly. "I'll be there in ten minutes."

Pryor sat on the sofa in the drawing room, waiting. She thought of the good time had in that room just a few hours earlier. She almost could hear the voices, the songs. She still could smell Miranda's perfume.

As promised, Egypt was there in ten minutes. When Pryor let her in she didn't speak. She looked at Pryor carefully, then led her to the drawing room where they sat together on the sofa. Pryor told her exactly what had happened. Egypt was astonished, then appalled. "A cord across the steps. An oldie but a goodie," she said grimly.

"I didn't know whether or not to call the police. I mean the family—"

"Yes, of course, the family. You don't want this in the newspaper or on TV." Egypt spoke drily.

"I was going to call Win."

''Do it.''

Pryor did. He didn't answer at first. Finally he spoke, his voice as distant and sleepy as Egypt's had been. There were no questions, just a promise to get there as soon as he could.

When Pryor returned to the drawing room, Egypt had poured two brandies. They sat again on the sofa, Persis between them.

''He's coming.''

''Good. Drink that. Shakespeare tells us that sleep knits up the raveled sleeve of care. I've always maintained that booze can knit up the raveled sleeve of anything.''

Pryor took a sip, choked, then took another. ''Who would do such a thing?'' she asked finally.

''Sugar''—Egypt pushed the hair from Pryor's eyes—''you're an heiress. Think first about money and who wants it most.''

''Surely you don't think that Miranda or Linda would be capable of wanting me dead.''

''As a matter of fact, I do. As well as Bruce and Cleve, both in financial binds. Fifty thousand dollars is a tidy sum but it pales beside three million.''

Pryor spoke sadly. ''We all had such a good time tonight. I felt they liked me, Egypt.''

''You're easy to like, sugar.''

"I'll be back in a minute." Pryor went to the kitchen, got a small dish of veal, and returned. Persis smelled it at once, leaped to the floor, and waited. She ate it daintily but swiftly. Pryor sat and finished half of her brandy.

When Win arrived, Egypt led him at once to the drawing room. He'd obviously thrown on some clothes, a tan sweater and khaki pants, sneakers. Pryor rose and he took both of her hands. "Are you all right, Pryor?"

"Yes." She was almost too exhausted to explain what had happened. She looked at Egypt beseechingly. Egypt recounted what had transpired then she led him to the stairs and showed him the nylon cord. He looked paler when they returned.

"And you didn't call the police?"

"No," Pryor assured him.

"We were thinking of the publicity," Egypt explained. "The family."

"Of course." He went to the drinks table, poured himself a straight scotch, and turned. "I know a sergeant on the force. Maybe he would just look into it for us." He returned to the sofa. "Is that all right with you, Pryor?" But Pryor, done in by the events of the evening and the brandy, looked at him hazily, slid sideways, and passed out.

Chapter Six

Before Sylvia was scheduled to appear with her breakfast tray, Pryor rose, dressed in white jeans and a white sweater, and went downstairs. She found Sylvia and Egypt drinking coffee at the kitchen table.

"Come join us," invited Egypt.

Pryor sat, eyeing Egypt's trim navy slacks and yellow shirt. "You're not going to work?" she asked.

Egypt stretched her long legs. "I'm taking my vacation," she said casually.

Sylvia poured Pryor some coffee, then sat beside her. There was a silence, as if all three of them were avoiding any discussion about the night before.

Finally Pryor spoke. ''I passed out, didn't I?''

Egypt laughed briefly. ''With grace and finality. I slept in one of the guest rooms, looked in on you several times. You were out cold.''

''Did Win's detective friend come?''

''You bet. He did the usual, took pictures, dusted for fingerprints, the works. He questioned both Win and me. He wants to see you today.''

Sylvia leaned toward Pryor. ''You want a little breakfast, child?''

''No, thank you, Sylvia.'' She turned to Egypt. ''What did the detective decide?''

Egypt shrugged. ''That Clemson was going to beat USC. Honey, they seldom decide anything off the bat, and if they do they don't tell you.''

''Thank you for staying the night, Egypt.''

''No sweat. Ma brought me some clothes.''

''No breakfast, honey?''

''Thank you Sylvia, but I think I'm going to get some fresh air.''

Despite their looks of surprise, Pryor, followed by Persis, went out the front door onto the piazza. The air smelled of the sea and some fragrant shrub. It was so peaceful Pryor couldn't credit what had happened the night before. She inhaled deeply, then went down the steps to the garden. The first thing she saw was a pile of dirt where the blighted fig tree had been. Then she saw darkly tanned arms lifting a shovel. Thomas Perrigeau was digging a hole for the magnolia tree he'd promised. It lay to one side, a healthy-looking specimen that would rise to about ten feet.

He saw her. At first he looked at her carefully, then put down his shovel, climbed out of the hole, and came toward her. He didn't take her hands in his. He offered no words of concern or sympathy.

"That's a very deep hole," she said.

Thomas looked at his handiwork. "The tree has unusually deep roots." He drew in an uneven breath. "About last night, Pryor—"

"Win had a detective friend come by. I didn't meet him. I sort of passed out."

"Understandable." He looked at her directly. "Any conjectures on your part?"

"No. Egypt says anyone in the family could be suspect. I can't believe that."

"Several people had a key to the house— Miranda, Linda, Win, Egypt, Sylvia, even I."

"How did you know what happened?"

"Egypt told Sylvia; Sylvia told Alice, Uncle Bubber's cook. She told Bubber and he told me."

They both watched Persis jump into the hole and sniff about. She pawed at the loose earth, ignored a seashell, pawed further.

"Persis the heroine," said Thomas. "We ought to have a medal struck."

"Or buy her a side of beef."

"I think she's dug up something. Bubber could be jealous. He hasn't found anything in days."

They watched the cat toy with whatever she'd found. Thomas knelt, then lowered himself into the hole. He disengaged Persis's treasure, held it up, and inspected it. After a few seconds he spoke. "I don't believe this!"

"What is it?" Pryor leaned over to see.

Thomas crawled out of the hole, held something toward her. It was covered with dirt, which she tried to brush away. They both looked at it without speaking. At last Thomas found his voice. "A Mickey Mouse watch," he said hoarsely.

There was no denying it. Pryor dropped the watch as if it were contaminated. Thomas picked it up, turned it over, inspected it carefully. ''I think,'' he said, ''it's time we call the police.''

Thomas went inside to phone. Pryor went to the kitchen where Sylvia was drying cups and Egypt stirring something at the stove. They turned to her at once. Sitting at the table, she told them what had been found in the garden.

They were silent, then Sylvia dropped a cup, but ignored it. ''Goodness gracious,'' she breathed. ''Miss Rosie.''

Egypt's response was louder, more cryptic. ''I'm not surprised.'' Carefully, she put down a wooden spoon.

Pryor waited in the library, staring at the shelves of books, a picture of young Althea and three little girls, Miranda, Linda, and Rosie. She was glad to be alone. She wished she was back in Overton, Pennsylvania. It was the middle of the morning. She might be having a cup of coffee or rearranging books, a dull day dwindling into a soothing duller night.

The police came, a youngish, heavyset sergeant and an even younger blond lieutenant. They questioned her at length, seeking information about her past and her present. They already knew about the cord across the step but they wanted her version.

A police crew busily dug further into the hole in the garden. She went twice to see what was happening. The second time Thomas stopped her on the piazza. "There's no point in sparing you," he said quietly. "They've found the remains. The teeth are being checked by a dentist who has her records." He took her arm, led her back to the door. "Pryor, pack a small bag and come with me. You can stay at Uncle Bubber's; there's plenty of room."

"Why?"

"I just don't think you're safe here, not until this thing is cleared up."

"Not safe? Just because somebody tried to kill me? Just because a body's been found in the garden?" Her voice rose, quavered.

"For now," the words came from the doorway, "you're going upstairs and have a nap. I'll take care of her, Thomas," said Egypt. "I'll be staying here nights."

She slept deeply, dreamlessly, curled up with Persis in her big bed. When she finally opened her eyes, she saw Egypt, looking down at her with an expression of pity and concern. "The troops are all downstairs," she said. "A family conference. I think they're waiting for you."

She braced herself with a shower, then put on a yellow cashmere sweater and skirt. She dreaded the confrontation. She was extra careful in going down the steps, Persis sailing ahead without a qualm.

She found them in the library, ensconced on the brown leather sofa and matching chairs. Linda wept untidily into a crumpled tissue. Miranda sipped from a strong drink, her face looking hollow but impassive. Their husbands stared uneasily into their drinks. Bruce looked as if he wanted to speak, Cleve as if he wished he were in Topeka or Vladivostock.

Pryor surprised herself with a calm, controlled voice. "I'm so very sorry."

Linda lifted her face from the crumpled tissue. "I just wish Mama could have known Rose didn't run off."

Miranda's tone was cold. "Consider the alternative. She hardly would have appreciated finding her six feet under in the garden."

Linda sobbed more loudly. Bruce cleared his throat. "The TV people will be here at any moment. We must decide what we're going to say."

"Yes," said Cleve, "a united front."

"Rosie," remarked Miranda, "would enjoy our saying that she always did the unexpected, was truly inventive."

"Darling," said Bruce levelly, "there's no need to be quite so unfeeling."

Miranda took a big drink. "Why be hypo-
crites? None of us was devoted to Rosie, you
know that. Incidentally, did the police, in all
their digging, find the diamond necklace and
bracelet?"

"No," said Cleve, his voice higher than
usual. "No sign of them."

"She had a lot of men friends." Miranda
handed her glass to Bruce for another drink.
"Heaven knows who was with her."

"He could have killed her, buried the body,
and taken off with the diamonds," said Cleve
eagerly.

"That hole in the garden, where the tree fell,
must have been very convenient," mused
Bruce.

Pryor, who was sitting on an ottoman near
Bruce, spoke to him directly. "I think the police feel it was an inside job."

They looked at her as if she'd uttered an
obscenity.

It was at that moment that Win Hazzard entered the room. He observed the gathering,
smiled at Pryor. "I've talked to the TV people," he said, "put them off, at least for the
moment. In the old days the family name would
have been a protection. Not any more, I'm

afraid.'' He addressed Pryor. ''Have the police come to any conclusions?''

''Not much,'' Pryor answered. ''They figure she was buried one or two days after the hurricane. Jacob remembers that he completely filled that hole on the third day after the storm. The murderer,'' she went on, ''added about three feet of soil, Jacob another three.''

Miranda nodded. ''There was a lot of rain after the hurricane. Everything would have sunk deeper, including Rosie.''

Sylvia entered with the large silver tea tray. Egypt, bearing another tray, followed with a platter of sandwiches, mugs of vichyssoise, and a plate of small pastries. Both left without speaking.

They ate as if starving or as an alternative to facing what had happened. There was no conversation except Linda's tentative suggestion that they all try to attend St. Michael's production of *Godspell*. Miranda admonished, ''Really, Linda.''

When Win rose from the sofa, where he sat between the two sisters, and offered his goodbyes, Pryor followed him to the front door. Once beyond the others' hearing, he turned to her. She was struck again by his handsomeness, his elegance.

"Pryor," he said quietly, "I hope you won't be intimidated by all this. I hope you'll stand your ground."

She loved his earnestness. "I'll try, Win. You can be sure of that."

He put his hands on her shoulders, looked at her intently. "Good girl." Then he was gone.

They seemed to drift away. It was Miranda who turned to her on the piazza and spoke with a trace of reluctance. "Listen, if there's anything we can do, please call us. Incidentally, you might consider staying with Bruce and me. This isn't exactly a tranquil house."

"I'll be fine, thank you. Egypt's going to be here."

With a wave of relief, Miranda went down the steps, sparing the briefest glance at the police workmen.

Chapter Seven

The days seemed to melt into each other. The police were no closer to finding Rose's murderer or whoever had placed the nylon cord on the steps. Egypt and Sylvia tried their best to cheer Pryor. Sylvia baked delicious cakes, pies, and muffins. Egypt found her excellent books to read. Win Hazzard took her out to dinner and dancing. She had danced but seldom. However, it was easy with Win, as smooth as their conversations. They talked about poetry, music, books. She discovered that Win had survived a lonely childhood, that he was more dominated by his Philadelphia father than his Charleston mother. Considering his impeccable manners, and courtliness, Pryor decided that his mother had her innings, as well.

He never came on to her in a precipitous or vulgar way, but she was aware that she attracted him. She decided that he was biding his time.

Thomas Perrigeau was out of town for several days. When he returned, he called at once, asking to be filled in on any new developments. Pryor informed him that there were none. He asked her to dinner with his Uncle Bubber and himself three days hence. She accepted.

Miranda called with another dinner invitation the following night. "Forgive the late call," she said, "it's just potluck. Bruce will pick you up about seven." Pryor insisted on driving herself; they argued, and Miranda finally acquiesced.

Wearing a pale gray silk pantsuit with gold buttons on the jacket and gold sandals, Pryor crawled into the old Mercedes and drove the six blocks to the Garner house. It was what the Charlestonians referred to as a single house, two rooms wide and four rooms deep, rising four floors. Painted a pale blue with green shutters, it had a walled garden to one side and a separate door leading to the piazza and front door.

Pryor knocked on the outside door and waited. Eventually it swung open and a young, uniformed maid led her down the piazza to the front door and inside. They went upstairs to a room where Miranda and Bruce sat in a close copy of Althea's library. They rose and greeted her, Bruce with a discreet hug, Miranda with a peck on the cheek.

''As I remember,'' said Bruce jovially, ''you like iced tea.''

''Fine.''

He made her a drink, refreshing Miranda's and his.

''Sit down, my dear.'' Miranda's voice was friendly as she led Pryor to the sofa. ''Bruce and I are a little ahead of you with our scotch. I'm not given to drinking but, everything considered, it seems to help.''

Miranda sat next to her and Pryor marveled at her sudden warmth, at the hand covering hers and the other hand shaking as it accepted a drink from Bruce.

Bruce finally sat and sighed. ''It's been a long day. Another interview with that police sergeant. They want to know the darnedest things, like my income, taxes, investments. Pryor, I suppose they've quizzed you as well.''

''Not about Rose, because I never knew her. About the attempt on my life, yes.''

Bruce sighed again. ''It just doesn't add up.''

Miranda shivered. "I feel we're at the mercy of someone very devious."

"But why kill Rosie?" Bruce shook his head. His face looked a bit haggard. "It doesn't add up," he repeated. "Rosie was to inherit everything, but so far as we know her death could have sent the estate to an animal shelter or the crisis ministry."

Miranda turned to Pryor. "No one knew you existed except Win."

"And Egypt," said Pryor.

"That hardly counts." Miranda shrugged and put her empty glass on the coffee table. "What a mess! I'm sick of the whole thing. Let's talk about something else."

They did. Miranda and Bruce described the changes in Charleston, the nouveau riche moving in with their lack of manners or values. They told Pryor about the Charleston they had known as children, the places they remembered, now gone.

"As my friend Ames observed," said Bruce sadly, "the Polish vodka and Brie cheese crowd has moved in."

Dinner was hardly potluck. There was cold cucumber soup, roast venison, potatoes au gratin, and two vegetables. Pryor found that she was hungry and enjoyed all of it. She particularly enjoyed Bruce saying that they were getting to be like the old guard and his recounting the story of a ninety-year-old woman who lived on Bedon's Alley. She was shocked by a young couple living there together out of wedlock. "It's not just what they're doing," she'd said, "but they're doing it in an old and historic district."

After dinner they sat again in the library, had their coffee, and looked at old family albums. Pryor saw pictures of her grandparents, great-grandparents, and adjacent relatives. Pryor's mother had not been interested in the past, so Miranda's stories of family trials and triumphs were particularly captivating. She loved the pictures of her mother and Althea, the latter looking much older but charmed by her little sister. She realized why Althea was partial to Rose, who not only looked like Alida but shared her joie de vivre.

All things considered, it was not a bad evening. She felt closer to Miranda and Bruce. They slowly seemed to be coming to accept her, to consider her family. Hard as it was, they must have resigned themselves to Althea's will.

Her next dinner party was with Thomas and his Uncle Bubber. "Very informal," said Thomas, "and Uncle's going to cook. He's

quite good, especially with local dishes. I'll be
by for you about six-thirty.''

He was prompt. She was glad she'd worn
black pants and a black chiffon blouse. Thomas
was dressed in a crisp, white shirt, tieless, with
khaki pants and polished loafers. He led her
next door and into a house filled with Victori-
ana. ''The eighteenth-century pieces are in the
Winston-Salem museum,'' he explained, ''sold
when the family fell upon evil times after the
War between the States.''

''I see.''

Bubber appeared, wearing an apron over his
neatly pressed pants. Like Thomas he was tieless but he'd added a red vest with gold buttons.
His thick curly hair was white; his face resembled a leprechaun's—eyes a brilliant blue below black brows like inverted V's, a small
pointed nose, a merry mouth. A small man, he
greeted Pryor with obvious pleasure, held her
hand between both of his.

''Welcome, my dear! What a pleasure! You
look a little like the Amorys but not too much.
Thank heaven, you don't have the family
blight.''

''What's that, Unc?'' asked Thomas,
grinning.

"An unfortunate overbite. She's lovely, Thomas."

Pryor didn't have time to be embarrassed. Bubber patted her on the shoulder and took off for the kitchen. Thomas poured martinis from a pitcher on an ornate desk. Eventually they sat on the Victorian sofa and chairs beneath eloquent Adam woodwork. Bubber had removed his apron and beamed at them.

"Thomas has told me something about you, my dear, but not enough. I want to know important things like your favorite authors, composers, religious beliefs, trees, birds and flowers, whether you credit the categorical imperative."

"Unc, leave her alone or give her a form to fill out. She's answered enough questions of late."

Bubber's face fell. "Of course, the police. The cord on the steps, poor Rosie."

"Exactly."

Bubber leaned over, took a cigar from a humidor on the coffee table and lit it while they watched. He blew out a stream of smoke. "I've been giving a lot of thought to the business about Rosie, the motives behind her death. I've discarded jealousy, envy, anger, and money. That leaves one possibility."

"What's that?" asked Pryor.

"Rosie knew something, threatened to tell it, to the murderer's chagrin."

No one spoke at once. Finally Pryor broke the silence. "The something she knew could have had to do with money."

"Beautiful *and* bright!" Bubber beamed at her.

"How can we possibly find out what it was?" asked Pryor, then sipped her martini.

"That will require more thought."

They went into the dining room to a dinner of fried shrimp, grits, and collard greens. It was delicious. Deliberately they abandoned the subject of Rosie. Bubber told amusing stories about what he described as "Charleston crackpots." He assured Pryor that he intended to become one. Pryor, thinking of the excavations in his garden, decided he'd *already* become one.

"I might put on a pirate costume," said Bubber, "and strut the battery as Stede Bonnet. He was hanged not far from here."

"Or drive down the middle of the street," added Thomas, "with your hand on the horn."

"That's been done."

Pryor took her leave at about eleven o'clock, not really wanting to go. She loved Uncle Bubber; she enjoyed Thomas. Yes, enjoy was the right word.

Thomas walked her to her door. ''Tell me,'' she said, ''who all had power of attorney to Aunt Althea's holdings?''

''Win, of course, as her lawyer, and Miranda and Linda.''

''Who paid the bills? Win?''

''No. Egypt. She wrote out the checks and Althea signed them.''

''You know an awful lot.''

''Althea and I were friends. She was very kind to me as a child, got me out of a lot of scrapes, sort of like a surrogate mother.''

''I see.''

At her front door Thomas stopped her. ''May I kiss you good night? Not a chaste peck but a real kiss?''

Pryor looked at his rough-hewn face, tumble of dark curls, the earnest eyes. ''I suppose so.''

''That's not what I'd call wild enthusiasm.''

''I'm sorry. I'm very tired.'' Trembling, she held up her face. Thomas patted her shoulder. ''I believe I'll wait for the wild enthusiasm.''

She lay in her bed and stared at the ceiling. Thomas kept coming between her and sleep. He was unlike any man she'd ever known, somehow freer. She could envision him in the Wild

West or at King Arthur's Round Table. Like his Uncle Bubber, he had an antic quality. He laughed at life. She wondered what would make him mad, what would incite him to passion. She decided to think about Win Hazzard and almost immediately fell asleep.

The next morning, after one of Sylvia's wonderful breakfasts, she asked Egypt who handled Aunt Althea's investments. Egypt looked in Althea's desk to be sure and reported Forest, Gray, and Winter. Pryor checked their number, phoned, and made an appointment for ten o'clock.

She dressed in a chic navy dress with a white collar and matching shoes, hoping to impress all the brokers with her dignity. Mr. Winter was a spare man in a three-piece suit. His scant hair was pulled to one side to cover a bald spot. To top things off, he wore rimless glasses and his thin lips rarely smiled.

Amazed at herself, Pryor threw back her shoulders, stared at him across a huge desk, informed him she was Althea Amory's heiress, and asked to know something about her holdings. Leonard Winter flushed, fumbled at his desk, and asked what she wanted to know. ''All the investments are completely safe,'' he said, "in tandems that are eighty-five-percent tax free."

"Can money be drawn from any of those tandems?"

"Yes. One. If needed."

"Did Althea draw much?"

"Occasionally. I believe it was for some of her charities."

"What was that tandem originally worth?"

Leonard Winter pushed a number of buttons on his computer and they both waited. At last he handed Pryor a piece of paper which showed the sum of five hundred thousand dollars.

"And how much is it worth now?"

More buttons were pushed. There was another wait. Finally he looked at her carefully, gave a smirk of a smile, and spoke. "Two hundred thousand dollars. The withdrawals were gradual."

"Thank you." She shook Leonard's clammy hand and hurried back to her Mercedes. Driving along the narrow streets she thought that Aunt Althea must have given three hundred thousand dollars to Rose, whom she adored or, as Leonard had said, to charities. But it didn't quite rest. Something was awry. Was Althea being blackmailed or was someone siphoning off those funds? Someone with power of attorney.

Win, Miranda, Linda, Egypt? Had Rose known?

As soon as she arrived home, she called Leonard Winter and asked the big question. Who had signed for that money? Again there was a long wait. She almost could hear him pushing buttons. When he spoke again, it was with consternation. "We don't seem to have a record of that. I can't explain why, except that we've had computer trouble over the years and some areas have been lost. I'm very sorry."

As she hung up, Egypt appeared and announced that lunch was ready. Pryor insisted that she, Egypt, and Sylvia eat together in the kitchen. They ate without much conversation, enjoying a wonderful minestrone soup, ham sandwiches, and salad. Pryor wished she could tell them what she had learned, get their opinion, but she was beginning to trust no one.

Instead she described her dinner with the Perrigeaus and Bubber's accounts of the Charleston crackpots.

"Oh, Mister Bubba." Sylvia laughed. "He knows this town like the back of his hand. Mister Bubba knows everything."

Not quite, thought Pryor grimly.

Chapter Eight

Pryor was a bit tired of being wined and dined, but when Linda called and in a hesitant voice asked her to supper, she knew she had to accept.

On the chosen night, Pryor took a long nap, had a long bath, and spent a long time surveying her acquired wardrobe. Egypt suggested a brown wool dress with a cowl neck and a wide gold belt. Pryor agreed.

She drove to the Martin house in a few minutes. It resembled Miranda's but was smaller. She peeked through the iron gates and saw an unweeded garden, grass that needed to be mowed. No maid answered the door. Cleve greeted her and led her inside. The room where they were to sit did not appear to be a drawing room. One might more accurately call it a parlor. The furniture was undistinguished, reproductions of eighteenth-century pieces. The proverbial sofa faced a fireplace, flanked by armchairs. There were two almost-empty bookshelves. Magazines open and facedown lay on tables and chairs. A pile of newspapers was stacked in one corner. It was not a messy room but held a look of disarray.

Cleve poured her an iced tea at an insubstantial-looking drinks table. He seemed honestly glad to see her. In his blazer and school tie he looked like a Yale senior at home for vacation. His wavy blond hair swept back from a high forehead, his eyes shone, and he had a perpetual smile. As he handed her the glass, Linda erupted into the room.

"Pryor, forgive me for not greeting you. I couldn't leave the potatoes." Her beruffled pink dress did little to flatter her overweight figure. There was a slight rip under one arm. But her rosy, sweating face was welcoming.

"That's all right, Linda. Cleve has made me feel quite at home."

Cleve paid no attention to his wife except to fix her a drink. They both sat close to Pryor on the sofa. It dawned on Pryor that the Martins had fortified themselves with several drinks. With each pressing close to her she tried to regain her aplomb. Linda spoke first.

"We're having a memorial service for Rose next Friday," she said. "It will be very simple. Afterward, people will call at Miranda's house."

Cleve cleared his throat. "The remains are to be cremated, as Rose stipulated in her will."

"She gave a great deal to charity," finished Linda. "Except the diamond necklace and bracelet, which she left to a friend."

"And which," said Cleve, "were never found."

Linda once more disappeared into the kitchen. Cleve offered Pryor another drink which she refused. They sat helplessly. The subject of Rose loomed so large, it blotted out alternatives. Cleve made a halting attempt at telling her some Charleston history. At one point she even found herself saying, "I declare."

Linda returned, even more flushed. "Dinner seems to be ready," she said uneasily.

They sat in a dining room furnished with Sheraton-reproduction table, chairs, and sideboard. They ate buffet, filling their plates at the

86   *Patricia Robinson*

sideboard. Seated, they began a meal of tough lamb chops, lumpy mashed potatoes, and underdone eggplant. Linda rose and went to the kitchen three times to get things she had forgotten—rolls, butter, and mint sauce. Conversation was sporadic. The only thing Pryor could praise with honesty was the dessert, an apple concoction.

"Huguenot torte," said Linda, pleased.

"It's not really Huguenot," said Cleve. "Years ago, a lady who ran a restaurant here snatched it from an old cookbook. It was called Arkansas pudding."

Pryor finished her last bite and pushed back her chair. "Whatever it is, it's delicious."

Linda refused Pryor's offer to help with the dishes and sent her back to the parlor with Cleve. Pryor, beset with boredom, pity, and a longing for bed, followed him.

Once again they sat on the sofa, Cleve too close.

"Poor little Pryor," he began. "I think of you a dozen times a day, going through all that horror, no one to turn to. What a rotten welcome to Charleston."

She couldn't say, "It's nothing, really," so she didn't say anything.

He moved even closer. ''If you need me for anything, anything at all, will you call me?''

''Sure. Thank you.''

''I saw Leonard Winter at lunch at the yacht club today and he said you'd been by for an appointment.''

There was a silence. Pryor knew she was expected to tell Cleve about the appointment but she was darned if she would.

''He's a nice fellow. I guess you wanted to talk about investments?''

''In a manner of speaking.''

''Pretty Pryor.'' He touched her cheek with one finger. ''I don't have Leonard's experience but I'd be glad to offer what expertise I have.''

She edged away, but he caught her hand. ''I've felt a real affinity with you, Pryor, since we met. We have a lot in common. Like being on the outside of this somewhat dysfunctional family.''

She suddenly realized that though he looked like a boy, there was a businessman inside, maybe inept but with the familiar thought processes. She rose abruptly, walked to the more than half empty shelves.

''Do you like to read?''

He looked surprised, chagrined. ''I do but there's not much time.'' He pointed to the stack of newspapers. "Those are *Wall Street Journals* I still want to go through."

"Pryor." He rose unsteadily and walked to her. "Don't feel guilty or uneasy about having a rapport with me. You can't destroy anything." He glanced toward the door. "There's nothing to destroy."

She never knew how she got through the rest of the evening. Linda returned and they engaged in mindless chatter. As early as she could, Pryor left, hurried to her car, and for a minute rested her head on her arms at the steering wheel.

Driving through the narrow streets with the elegant lighted houses, she considered forfeiting her inheritance, leaving town as soon as possible. She'd never belong here. She felt threatened, somehow imperiled. She'd never been greedy and knew she was not greedy now. It was not the money that held her. It was something else, a gut-deep stubbornness in the face of shifting dangers.

When she reached her house, it looked oddly menacing, full of secrets. She got out, walked slowly to the door. The figure came from the shadows. For a moment she was terrified. Thomas looked down at her. "I just wanted to make sure you got home all right."

''How did you know I'd gone?''

''Your car was missing. Was it a marvelous evening?''

''It was dreadful.'' They sat together on the top step and she told him about her dinner with Linda and Cleve, especially the way Cleve flirted with her.

''Why, that little wimp!''

''In a way it was funny.''

''I suppose so. And I suppose you think that all these gents flattering you—Win, Cleve, me— is because of your money.''

''It's crossed my mind.''

''Pryor, have you ever really looked at yourself? You're beautiful. I don't know about the other two, but *I* already have plenty of money. You know, since I've met you, I've discovered another side of myself, a rightness, an inevitability, a recognition.'' He stood up, angry with himself. ''I don't know exactly how to put it. I make a living with words and, suddenly, words fail me.'' He started down the steps. ''As my old nurse used to say, 'Sleep sweet, darlin'.' ''

Pryor stumbled after him. He caught her before she fell. ''Thomas.'' She said the word as if it were a blessing. ''Hold me.'' She lifted her face. ''You said it all perfectly. You—'' His lips were on hers in a kiss that was long and deep, and somehow inevitable. He pulled away abruptly. "I'm sorry, Pryor."

The next morning at ten o'clock Thomas, Egypt, and Pryor sat at the kitchen table drinking coffee. In careful detail Pryor told the other two about her meeting with Leonard Winter, including the fact that Leonard could find no record of who had made large withdrawals from Althea's account. "And there's no way we can find out," Pryor finished.

"Looks that way," said Egypt glumly.

"Not exactly." Thomas was rubbing his chin.

"What do you mean?" asked Pryor.

Thomas settled back in his chair. "All we have to do is get a look at savings accounts, see who deposited what and when."

Egypt took a sip of coffee. "But that's confidential, isn't it?"

Thomas grinned. "To a newspaperman, nothing is really confidential."

Pryor leaned toward him. "You mean you really could find out?"

"It may take a while, but I have means. And friends," he added.

Egypt rose. "Thomas," she spoke with admiration, "are you really such a sneaky con artist?"

"When the occasion demands it."

Egypt blew them a kiss and left.

Pryor and Thomas looked everywhere but at each other. She wondered if he regretted the night before.

He didn't speak at once. He took her hand, turned it over, and kissed the palm. He looked into her eyes. "Don't worry. We'll clear this up. And please don't worry about what I said last night."

She didn't answer. She watched him get up and leave the room.

Chapter Nine

For several days very little happened. She read some of the books Egypt had given her, she napped, she walked around the lovely old town with Thomas, staring at the incredible houses. He told her informative and amusing stories of the people who lived in them. There was no repeat of the late-night scene on her steps, except in the way he looked at her, touched her arm, called her each morning.

She couldn't think of him without a shiver of delight. She knew now why she had stayed in Charleston. Thomas was the essence of all her dreams. Nothing might come of their encounter, but at least she had here and now. True to form, she expected nothing but was grateful to know what she was capable of feeling.

Win called when she and Egypt were going over some household accounts. He suggested supper at his house. "There will be some people you'll enjoy, Pryor. Two of my best friends."

She couldn't think of a good excuse to decline. She hemmed and hawed a little, and then accepted. As soon as she hung up, Egypt burst into laughter. "That man always gets what he wants and something tells me he wants you, Pryor."

"Don't be silly."

"He's one handsome devil. You must admit that."

"I do. But he's not my type."

"Thomas maybe is." Pryor didn't reply.

"Thomas," mused Egypt, "he must be thirty or so and as far as I know he doesn't give the time of day to any girl."

"Egypt, the gas and electric bill seems awfully high."

She insisted on driving herself to Win's. Going through the old streets at night gave the town an enchanted look. Part of it was the history. Since she'd first come to Charleston, despite the horror and confusion, she'd had a sense of unreality, of being distanced from the rest of the world.

Win lived in a double house, huge and imposing. There was no false door leading to a piazza, but an impressive entrance with a big brass knocker.

An elderly man in butler's garb answered the door, ushered her into a hall leading to a double staircase, then into a room with a small fire crackling on the hearth. There were books, hunting prints, and furniture covered with a dark, attractive material. The room held an air of comfort, ease without attempting to be imposing.

Win walked from before the fireplace to greet her. She noticed at once his look of strain. His handsome face didn't sag but there were lines she hadn't noticed before.

"Pryor, I must apologize for my other guests. They won't be coming. One of their youngsters seems to be suffering from measles. Josh and Maggie are very diligent parents. In this case, no sitters will do. Come, dear, sit down. You must indulge me with the fire. It's not cold but I find it cool."

She sat on the sofa. "I love a hearth fire."

"Friends tell me I have one if the temperature goes below seventy.'' They both laughed uneasily.

Win went to a bar at the other side of the room, fixed her a drink. For the first time she noticed a lack of smoothness, evidence that something was bothering him.

They sat with their drinks, holding a rather formal conversation. Pryor commented on some artifacts—a small Cambodian statue, antique paperweights, a Russian lacquered box. Win explained their history and provenance. It was Pryor who mentioned the memorial service to be held for Rose.

''Yes.'' Win spoke slowly. ''The girls have asked me to give a eulogy. I've never done anything like that but Rose was my friend.''

He got up, walked to the mantel, took a long drink. His hand holding the glass shook a little.

She suddenly felt very sorry for him. Something was bothering him and it wasn't Rose or the eulogy.

Finally she couldn't stand it. ''Win,'' she said gently, ''what is it? What's troubling you? I don't mean to intrude, but you're just not yourself.''

''It's nothing really.'' His face flushed; he took another drink. ''I'm just a little tired, had a rough day.''

"We haven't known each other long, but I feel we're friends. Won't you admit that much, let me try to help you?"

He put his glass on the mantel. "I'm afraid there's nothing either of us can do." He sat beside her on the sofa, looked at her squarely. "I've been close to the Amorys for years. In a way they've been like my family. When I first came here from Philadelphia I knew no one, had no friends. Althea more or less took me in."

"I'm glad."

"I spent holidays with them, lived through their happy times and crises with them."

"I'm sure you were also a big help."

"When I could be."

Pryor hesitated then dared to ask, "What's happened, Win?"

He too hesitated, then took a deep breath. "Last night at a party I overheard two men discussing the Amorys. One of them was Bruce's best friend." He took another breath, looked away from her. "It seems that before she died Rose was often seen with Bruce, Miranda's husband."

Neither of them said a word. The fire crackled.

"I can't believe it," breathed Pryor.

"If the police get wind of this Bruce will be in real trouble."

"You mean a crime of passion?"

"Possibly."

"Or," said Pryor carefully, "it could mean she knew something he wanted to cover up."

Win didn't answer. He put his head in his hands. Pryor longed to comfort him, put her arms around him, but she didn't want to give him the wrong idea.

It was at this moment that the butler announced dinner. The two of them sat at a long, candlelit table, eating little of the delectable meal. Pryor sensed that Win wanted to be left alone. After dinner, as soon as she could, she pleaded a headache and, followed by Win, went to the hall to get her purse and coat. After he'd helped her into her coat, she turned to him, touched his cheek.

"Win, get some rest. You can't worry about the whole Amory family."

He held her hand to his cheek. "Thank you, Pryor." He saw her to her car, watched as she drove away.

She didn't go directly home. She drifted along the streets, trying to collect her thoughts. It seemed downright evil that Rose would get involved somehow with her brother-in-law. But

Rose seemed to have made her own rules. She tried to envision Bruce as a murderer, but failed.

She lay awake for a long time, thinking about Bruce and Rose. It was hard to fathom. She could imagine Cleve as a cad because of the way he'd flirted with her. But Bruce, the impeccable Charleston gentleman with so much to lose? She thought about Win, devoted to the family. He seemed so lonely and isolated. She could understand his devotion to the Amorys. Lastly, she let herself think of Thomas. She went over his attributes in her mind—the tall, bronze athlete's body, the dark curls, the rugged face with tender eyes. Sleep evaded her. She began to wonder if she were safe. The memory of the cord across the step prompted her to think of being alone. She thought of being in the house at night without Egypt. She slid out of bed and barefoot, followed by Persis, padded soundlessly to the guest room next door.

She not only saw Egypt in the big bed but saw her sit up at once, switch on a light. They stared at each other.

"You all right, sugar?"

"Yes. I was just checking to make sure you were here. I had an odd evening with Win Hazzard and it kept me awake."

Egypt giggled. ''An evening with Win Hazzard would keep any girl awake. He flirted?''

''No.''

''Too bad. Why odd?''

''Something he told me.''

Egypt patted the bed, motioned to Pryor to sit beside her. Gratefully, Pryor sat. Unhappily she repeated what Win had said. Egypt gasped.

''That can't be true! Bruce and Rose!''

''Do the police know anything more, Egypt?''

''They know the teeth match Rose's dental records. And there's a mark on the skull that shows she could have been hit.''

Pryor shivered. Egypt patted her hand. ''Two pieces of advice, sugar. Don't trust anybody, and this is no time to fall in love. It clouds the mind.''

''Oh, Egypt.''

''Another thing we know for sure.''

''What's that?''

''Whoever put that cord on the stairs has a key to the house. That's quite a few people.''

Once again Pryor shivered. Egypt got out of bed, stretched. ''What do you say we go down and make some cocoa?''

''I say hurrah.''

*   *   *

The next morning while dressing, she carefully considered her options. She could go back to Overton and forget the whole business. She could barricade herself in her room with an armed guard. She could proceed with caution but courage, believing Rose's murder would be solved as well as the mystery of the cord across the steps. She opted for the last. She'd been timid too much of her life. She would not be timid now. Picking up her purse, she went downstairs.

She found Egypt and Thomas in the kitchen eating the pancakes Sylvia flipped onto their plates. She sat with them, accepting coffee, but declined breakfast.

"Thomas," she said, "have you found out anything at all? Were you able to uncover anything about deposits in savings accounts?"

"Not yet. It may take another day or two, but I'll keep at it."

She asked Sylvia about groceries that were needed. Egypt spoke up quickly. "I'll get them, Pryor. I've got the list."

"But I want to get out, drive around."

Reluctantly Egypt gave her the list. Pryor put it in her purse, rose, and started through the dining room. Thomas followed. She decided that his arm around her was more protective than amorous. Outside, they stopped on the piazza steps and looked down at the deep, wide hole. Pryor shivered, realized she'd been shivering a lot. And fainting. Well, not exactly. One of the incidents had been a simple passing out.

''I think,'' said Thomas, ''that the police dug further, hoping to find the necklace and bracelet. They've given up, decided the killer took them.''

It was starting to drizzle. Thomas pulled her onto the piazza. ''Let me get the groceries for you. Give me the list.''

''No. But thank you.''

''Can't I at least get you an umbrella?''

''There's one in the car.''

Without waiting for a reply she went out the piazza door and hurried down the steps. Her car was parked directly behind Egypt's red Nissan. Hurriedly, she unlocked the door and climbed in. She already was damp but not sodden. She started the car and went down the street. The drizzle of rain had turned into a downpour. Pryor turned on the windshield wipers and headed for East Bay Street. She went several blocks, peering ahead through the wash of water. She'd heard about sudden tropical storms and this was the proof.

It was a few seconds later that the cat, a Si-amese like Persis, edged from sidewalk to street and ran directly into her path. She braked the car. Nothing happened. She braked again. There were no brakes. In a panic she veered to the right, felt the car go out of control. She almost hit a fireplug, missed it by inches. The next thing she knew the car crashed head-on into a telephone pole. The impact was loud, jolting, shaking her badly. She sat dazed, her hands on the wheel. People appeared at windows and then ran into the street. Cars stopped behind her. She was aware of someone opening the car door, peering in at her—an older man, his face full of concern.

"Are you all right?"

"Yes," she said. "I think so."

The rain poured down his face, blurred his glasses. "Let me help you." He freed her from the seat belt, gently assisted her from the car. With a small crowd watching, he led her into his house, directly in front of them.

She was next aware of being led to a sofa where the man suggested she stretch out. He put a pillow under her head. She closed her eyes to avoid further conversation. She heard a police siren. The man asked her for a home number to call. She told him.

It seemed that Thomas and Egypt were there at once. After being assured that she was all right, they thanked the old man and, one on either side, helped her from the room.

"Stubborn lil' missy," said Egypt, sounding just like her mother.

Once at home, she immediately was put into bed, given a shot of brandy and then a cup of herbal tea. The three of them stood at the foot of the bed and stared at her with deep concern.

"It was the brakes," she said weakly. "The brakes didn't work." Thomas and Egypt exchanged a glance.

"I know it's an old car," said Pryor. "I probably should have had it checked."

Thomas left the room abruptly. "I had it checked," said Egypt. "Everything was fine."

Sylvia and Egypt insisted that she rest and, if possible, sleep. Persis curled beside her.

Amazingly, she slept. She slept through lunch and on into the evening. She awoke when Egypt brought a tray with a tempting dinner.

"I talked to the police," Egypt said. "No charges filed. Your car's been towed away."

Pryor finished her meal and at once went back to sleep.

*   *   *

It was Thomas who came the next morning and told her what had caused the wreck. She was still in bed, finishing a cup of coffee and feeding Persis some bacon. When she saw him she couldn't help being glad that she was wearing a hand-embroidered nightgown.

"It was not your fault, Pryor. There was no brake fluid. Nor was there a leak."

"What does that mean?"

"It means someone removed, maybe siphoned off, the fluid." His face was grim. "If you'd been going any faster it would have been far worse. Thank heaven for the rain."

I'm not going to shiver, thought Pryor, but she did.

"Pryor, please come and stay with Uncle Bubber and me. Two women alone in a house is not a good idea."

"No. I'm going to stay here."

"You are one darned stubborn woman!" He half grinned.

"Thomas, I have a feeling we're getting very close to something."

"Maybe too close."

She started to get out of bed but stopped, realizing she still felt weak. "Thomas, look in the left drawer of the desk. It may be nothing of importance, but you might have an opinion."

He moved quickly, retrieved Rose's scratch pad, and stared at it.

"What do you think?"

"I think it could be of considerable importance."

Thomas had told the police about the absence of brake fluid and they'd confirmed this at the service station. By the time they came to question her, Pryor was dressed and in cold control of herself. Sitting in the drawing room, answering their queries, she felt surprisingly remote. The fact that someone wanted her dead had sunk in and produced a kind of deep resistance.

After the police left, Thomas appeared and pulled her to her feet. He looked at her stylish paisley dress.

"Go and put on some old clothes. I think you need a change of scene."

She didn't question him about where they were going. Obediently she went up to her room, dressed in jeans, a sweater, and sneakers. They drove in Thomas's old van, across the town and over a bridge. He spoke little. At last he turned to her. "You've seen a bit of Charleston; it's time you saw something of the Low Country." They passed shopping centers and housing developments and suddenly they were in open land. Marsh and wide savannas stretched on either side as they went down a highway. At last they turned to the right, then proceeded along a narrow paved road. At what seemed the end of this, they went onto an even narrower dirt road for several miles. Pryor was aware of ancient oaks with Spanish moss, scrub trees, and tall reeds. They drew up beside what looked like an inlet. On the bank lay an overturned canoe. Thomas helped her from the van, uprighted the canoe, dragged it into the water, moored it, and loaded it with the things he'd brought, a picnic basket and a blanket. He helped her into the prow of the canoe, seated himself at the stern, and pushed away from the land. He used the oar skillfully as they went down the creek.

She saw frogs jumping, a white egret taking off and flying into the trees. She even saw an alligator.

"Look," he whispered. Just ahead was a fawn stopping for a drink of water.

She hardly breathed, so entranced with the wildlife all around her. Nothing else existed. She saw snakes, possums, racoons. The water was dark, mysterious, seeming to hold another world of unseen creatures. Even the air smelled different.

After about two miles Thomas steered the canoe to a bank. Here he got out, moored the boat, and helped her to the land. He spread the blanket in a small glade and added the picnic basket. They sat without speaking for several minutes.

''I see what you mean,'' she said finally.

''Bubber and I used to come here when I was a boy. He taught me about wildlife, how to paddle a canoe. Sometimes we went fishing.''

Pryor could imagine him as a boy, with tousled dark curls, his sturdy little body darkly tanned. He would have had the same look of wonder his eyes held now.

''Is Bubber the only family you have left?''

''Of close family, yes. When he goes I'll be alone.'' It was not said with self-pity, just as fact.

They ate a lunch of shrimp sandwiches, gazpacho, and fresh fruit. Thomas opened a bottle of wine.

It wasn't until the sun was beginning to set that they reloaded the canoe and headed back. She wanted to thank him for sharing a part of his world. She couldn't find the words.

Chapter Ten

Pryor was getting a bit tired of surprises, but she couldn't help being pleased when mousy Linda called and asked her to go riding. It turned out that the riding was on horseback and the invitation offered so hesitantly that Pryor found herself accepting.

In her closet where she went for pants and a sweater, Egypt found some new well-fitting jodhpurs, jodhpur boots, and a tweed riding jacket. Aunt Althea had truly thought of everything.

Linda called for her at ten in a Toyota that had passed its prime. Once again Pryor left the town behind and was in the country. Linda, in well-worn riding clothes, drove without much talking. At last Linda ventured a remark.

"I'm glad you like horseback riding, Pryor."

Pryor didn't want to say that it was new territory for her, so she hedged. "I haven't had much opportunity, but I'm looking forward to it." She changed the subject. "What's that green berry, Linda?"

"It's holly, not yet ripe." As they went down a dirt road she pointed out pyracanthas, wisteria vines, and huge camellia bushes growing wild and covered with buds. They saw a raccoon, several deer, and a possum. Linda identified jaybirds, mockingbirds, Carolina wrens, woodpeckers, falcons, and hawks.

Quite suddenly, they came to a large brick house. It looked weathered and quite old, and beyond it was a huge barn which Linda said was the stable.

"The horses aren't mine," Linda was quick to explain. "They belong to an old school friend. She loves to have them exercised."

"I hope mine is tame, lazy, and good tempered."

"She is. You won't have any trouble."

They found the horses already saddled by an elderly, almost toothless man who greeted Linda with a hug. He looked askance at the basket she carried. "Can you manage that and Prince, too?"

"You bet I can, Oscar. This is my friend, Pryor. I think Stella is ideal for her."

Pryor looked at the brown mare staring listlessly at the ground. She appeared incapable of rebellion.

Once mounted they proceeded slowly down a lane. Linda reined in Prince to keep pace with Pryor, whose mount was in no hurry. They went for some minutes and Pryor found that she was enjoying herself. At last Linda and Prince broke into a trot and Pryor found herself following, remembering how to post. She was amazed at how well Linda rode. She looked like she'd been born on a horse. And she looked supremely happy. Her cheeks were rosy and her eyes shone.

It took Pryor quite a while to register the fact that she was on horseback in South Carolina having a very good time and well distanced from fear and distrust. She found herself smiling as they went down the lane, bordered by tall pines and spreading oaks.

It must have been over an hour when Linda stopped, slid off the saddle, and tethered Prince to a low hanging branch. Pryor did the same. They were in a glade beside a narrow creek.

Linda spread a plaid blanket and put her basket in the middle. Charlestonians seemed to love picnics. She motioned to Pryor to sit. The nervousness she displayed in her own house was gone. She poured tea from a thermos for them and handed Pryor a plate of sandwiches. She was not given to talk, used to being alone on most of her rides, but at last she looked at Pryor squarely and spoke. ''Thank you for coming today. I didn't think you would.''

''Why wouldn't I, Linda? This is fun.''

''After all the things that have happened to you I thought you might be afraid.''

''Afraid?''

''Of another accident. That I might spook your horse.''

''It never occurred to me.''

''No. I don't think it did.'' Linda stared at her sandwich. ''You're a very nice person, Pryor, and I asked you today because I wanted to offer a part of myself that counts. My riding. I wanted to share it with you. No one but Cleve and the woman who owns the horses knows about it.''

''Does Cleve ride?''

''Occasionally. Usually when he feels he should be nice to me, like when he's been mean to me.''

Pryor was shocked at the matter-of-factness but she made no comment.

"Haven't you wondered why a handsome, charming man like Cleve should marry a dull dormouse like me? No, don't answer. I'm sure you have. Well, I think it's because he knew I'd put up with whatever he did." She put down the sandwich, looked toward the creek.

Finally Pryor couldn't stop herself. She blurted it out. "Linda, why do you stay with him?"

There was a silence. They both sipped their tea. When Linda, spoke her voice was calm.

"My grandmother gave me a piece of advice I've never been able to forget. 'Keep your promises, your vows,' she said. 'The important thing is to live with honor.' " Her laugh was sudden, empty. "I may be a mess but I've tried to live with honor."

Added to Pryor's astonishment was the thought that the word "honor" was seldom used. She didn't know how to reply.

She decided to take advantage of Linda's openness. "Linda, it's none of my business, but was Bruce involved with Rose in any way? Somebody told me he was."

Linda's smile was enigmatic. "I don't know

about Bruce, but she was seen having lunch with Win. And, of course, Cleve . . .''

Pryor decided to let this go, but she couldn't. ''What about Thomas Perrigeau?''

''Oh, Thomas.'' She laughed. ''As far as I know he walks alone. Rose once remarked that he had childish dreams and impossible standards.'' She turned suddenly and regarded Pryor. ''Are you interested in him?''

''Not really. Just curious.'' She returned the glance. ''Linda, are you happy?''

Once again Linda looked toward the creek. ''Happy? No. It's not within my frame of reference. I'm content. I survive. By the time I was sixteen I decided that survival was the most I could hope for. Does that shock you?''

''No. I had somewhat the same experience.''

Pryor thought of the dreariness of her life in Overton, the lonely, endless weekends, the vacations spent by herself at the Chautauqua festival. She thought of her girlish dreams of the proverbial knight. She thought of those dreams diminishing into someone just to be home for, to hold her and be there for her. She was deeply curious about Thomas Perrigeau's impossible standards but she refrained from asking Linda more.

''Thomas,'' mused Linda, ''is truly kind, has

always been. In the old days, when forced to go to dancing school, you never worried about being a complete wallflower. Thomas would certainly ask you to dance, no matter what you looked like.''

''Yes,'' said Pryor weakly, wondering if Thomas saw her as another wallflower. ''What about his parents?''

''His mother died when he was young. I don't know about his father. He grew up at his Uncle Bubber's house.''

Pryor longed to help this woman, somehow to help her toward a better image of herself. She didn't know where to begin. With herself, she thought grimly. With Linda's perception of her, flawed but worth achieving.

''Well, we'd better start back.'' Linda began packing the basket, Pryor helping.

When they were again mounted, Linda turned to her. ''Pryor, forgive me for using you as a sounding board. I guess I needed to unload on someone who was, well, not judgmental.''

''I'm very flattered, Linda.''

''I think—I hope—that we're going to be friends.''

Pryor smiled at the rosy face. ''I think that we already are.''

They spoke little on the ride back to the barn,

less on the trip down the highway to town. When Pryor turned to get out of the car, she turned back, kissed Linda on the cheek, and hurried into her house.

Sylvia helped Pryor into a warm bath, insisting on rubbing her arms and legs with Absorbine Jr. "So's you won't be stiff tomorrow." The next thing Pryor knew, she was wearing a butter-yellow housecoat, more like a dinner dress, sitting in a wicker chair on the piazza, and sipping lemonade. She didn't really want to be on the piazza. She could see the big hole in the ground. She shuddered.

Before she could leave, the piazza door swung open and Thomas stepped in.

"Just wanted to say hello." In a gray pinstriped suit, shirt, tie, and polished shoes, he looked like a banker. Noticing her surprised appraisal, he grinned. "I'm on my way to meet the editor of a magazine about a story on Northern Ireland. I'm going to turn her down, but she's an old friend."

"Why turn her down?"

Thomas leaned against the piazza railing. "I guess I'm having war-and-disaster burnout. I guess I've had enough of wailing widows, starving children, and people lying dead in the street." His face looked years older.

"What will you do?" she asked.

"Stay home. Write another book. Dig for artifacts with Bubber."

"Well, at least you have plans."

"What are *your* plans? A schloss in Austria, a houseboat in Katmandu, a villa on the Riviera?"

"I might plant a garden."

"So Charleston and the Low Country have cast their spell."

"What do you mean?"

"A place that enchants, bedazzles, that lies somewhere between myth and reality."

"With someone's remains in the garden. Have you discovered anything else?"

"I'm working on it."

She didn't press this further, took another direction. "Someone told me you have impossible standards where women are concerned. Is that true?"

"Rose used to say that." He looked at the hole. "Poor vivid Rosie."

Pryor smoothed her shirt.

"I suppose I do have impossible standards."

"What are they?" she asked bluntly.

Hands in pockets, he leaned on the rail, regarded her. "Honest, kind, trustworthy, faithful, prone to laugh, and compassionate with children and animals.''

It was at that moment that Sylvia appeared in the doorway to the house. She glanced toward Thomas. ''Mister Tommy, are you stayin' to supper?''

He stood erect, smiled, shook his head. ''No, Sylvia, I'm being wined and dined by a beautiful, untrustworthy, faithless, laughless woman, noted for a dislike of children and animals.'' Before either could reply, he was out of the piazza door.

Win called and suggested a last-minute supper. She gracefully declined. After vichyssoise and a salad she went to her room, followed by Persis.

She was not only surprised but astonished when Miranda appeared late the next afternoon. As usual she looked beautiful and svelte and she carried a fairly large box. She didn't swan into the drawing room but walked hesitantly, as if her visit might be an imposition. Once they were seated together on the sofa, she handed Pryor the box.

''It's not much,'' she said, ''but I wanted to give you something of my own.''

Pryor opened the box, found inside its tissue wrapping a ceramic figure about six inches tall.

A man, holding a skull in his long, sensitive hands, was incredibly handsome, with blond hair and a high-cheekboned face that was both wry and sad. Hamlet. Ophelia was next, lovely in a flowered dress, already with a hint of madness. Last was Polonius, plump, a bit ostentatious, a bit confused.

Pryor stared at them, lined up on the coffee table. "Miranda," she breathed, "they're incredible. And you made them yourself?"

Miranda's laugh was short, self-deprecating. "I've been fooling around with clay for years."

"Has anyone in your family seen these?"

"Only Bruce. He was unimpressed until I sold some through a gift shop."

"They should be sold through a jeweler," said Pryor. "They're exquisite."

"You really think so?" It was almost a plea.

"I certainly do." She spoke next without thinking. "How could Bruce fail to see that?"

"Oh, you mustn't blame Bruce. I don't think he looked at them too carefully." She took a cigarette from her purse and lit it. "I hope you like Bruce. He certainly likes you."

"Of course." Pryor neither liked nor disliked Bruce. But she wondered about his relationship with Rose. "I'm sure your mother was pleased when you married him."

"I think she felt we deserved each other, both dull, both predictable. Mama preferred people who were mysterious and a bit antic."

"Like Rose?"

"Yes. In her eyes Rose could do no wrong." She looked toward a window. "Bruce was inclined to agree with her."

"But he married you."

"I've always wondered if I was second choice," said Miranda. She turned back to Pryor, smiled. "Not that it matters."

Pryor touched her hand. "I think he made a very good choice."

They talked of other things. Miranda explained how she made the figurines. "First I model them in clay," she explained, "fire them in my kiln, then color them and fire them again. If I use gold or silver, I fire them a third time."

"A lot of work."

"Not really. Next I plan to do Othello, Desdemona, and Iago."

"You stick to Shakespeare?"

"Not really. I've done things like the Snow Queen and the Pied Piper." She stood. "Pryor, I've got to leave. I didn't mean to stay so long."

"I've loved seeing you. And I'll treasure my little figures."

After Miranda had left, Pryor studied the figures, turned them over in her hand. She marveled at Miranda's creativity. She was putting them on the mantel when Egypt came in. Egypt studied Miranda's offering, shook her head.

"You never know about people, do you?"

"No."

"I mean, we tend to stick to first perceptions."

"Exactly."

"My first marriage was when I was eighteen. I saw Manuel as a combination of St. Peter and Abe Lincoln, with a little Bill Cosby thrown in. Rugged, good-looking, a sense of humor. He was something! But by the time I was twenty I couldn't wait to get rid of him. He not only hit me but took all the money I made as a waitress. As Mama said, he was half in and half out the door, a can full of worms. Talk about first perceptions!"

"What are you trying to tell me, Egypt?"

"Don't trust first perceptions, or second and maybe not third."

"You're talking about my relatives."

"I'm trying to save your life."

"Oh, Egypt."

"Night and day I'm trying to figure out who put the cord across the steps, who drained the fluid from the brakes, who has a key to the house, who has the most to gain. All I've got are conjectures. It's someone close, methodical but imperfect. It's someone who will try again.''

''You're beginning to scare me.''

''I hope so. That's why I'm staying here with you. A witness is the last thing they want.''

''When your husband left, what did you do?''

''That's when your Aunt Althea helped me through college and law school.''

''Dinner's ready.'' Sylvia stood importantly in the doorway.

Pryor took her plate into the kitchen and ate with Egypt and Sylvia. They talked mostly of Althea, who was idolized by Sylvia and Egypt.

''She was one fine lady,'' said Sylvia.

''So I gather,'' spoke Pryor. ''I wish I'd known her.''

''When she read reports of you she said, 'This is the daughter I should have had.' ''

It suddenly occurred to Pryor that in her recent encounters with Linda and Miranda, both had been somewhat defensive.

Chapter Eleven

Rose's memorial service was held at St. Michael's church, with a sizeable gathering. Along with the well-dressed Charlestonians, Pryor saw several odd characters and a few curious tourists. All of Sylvia's family were present.

There were prayers and hymns and then Win went to the pulpit. As usual he looked elegantly handsome, but drawn and pale. His eulogy was eloquent. He talked of Rose's beauty, her warmth and generosity, her joie de vivre, sense of humor. It was short, vivid. And as he said the final words, ''We shall not see her like again,'' he was noticeably choked up.

After the service a great many people went to Miranda's house. It was like a big cocktail party—drinks, and a wide selection of hors d'oeuvres. With her drink, Pryor stood on the piazza watching the festivities. She was shocked. It was like a celebration. Thomas appeared at her side and held out a small sandwich. "Try this. They're good."

She shook her head. "I can't get over this. It's barbaric."

"No. It's Charleston." He ate the sandwich. "You'll find that most manners here are based on a consideration of others. Also, it's the way Rose would have wanted it. If they cry, they'll cry later at home."

"Was Rose popular?"

"Yes. She always livened things up, made people feel good. She made women feel interesting and men important."

"And you?"

"I liked her because she brought light into Althea's life. I was younger than she, but she made me feel like a man of the world, even when I was a callow, bumbling youth."

"Aren't these people shocked at the way she died?"

"Yes. But in another way, I don't think anyone who really knew her expected that she'd die in a normal way. On a ski slope maybe, or a public disaster. Of course, murder is a bit outré.''

''It's a horror.''

''Yes.'' He looked down at her, held her shoulders.

''Oh, Thomas.''

A couple, passing them, looked on with interest then moved away.

Two women came out on the piazza and dragged Thomas away. Pryor thanked Miranda, got her purse from the hall, and was heading across the sidewalk to her car when Win Hazzard ran out of the house and stopped her. ''Pryor, dear, I've wanted to talk to you but old Jem Calder had me barricaded in the dining room.'' He looked more relaxed, more like his old self. ''In a few days, I'm obliged to go to Serena Blackshear's debut, something I can't refuse. Would you be an angel and come as my date?''

Pryor grappled in her mind for excuses to refuse but found nothing credible. ''Thank you, Win, I'd like that.''

The few days went swiftly. Egypt was ecstatic. ''Wonderful! That will be a real bash, something you've got to see. And don't tell me you've nothing to wear. You've a closet full of possibilities.''

She and Egypt argued for three days about what she was to wear. She preferred something understated, Egypt a confection. Egypt, backed by Sylvia, won. On the day of the party, she was allowed by her mentors to take a walk on the battery, eat a light lunch, and then was ordered to take a nap and a long luxurious bath.

Sylvia and Persis watched as Egypt lifted the dress over Pryor's head and zipped up the back. They all gasped. Strapless with a delicately tucked bodice, it swirled out in yards of pale peach chiffon over petticoats of starched net. It was technically simple but visually dazzling. Egypt had brushed her red-blond hair until it shone, curled inward on her shoulders.

''No jewelry,'' said Sylvia. ''It doesn't need jewelry.''

''A small tiara would be nice,'' mused Egypt.

''My pearls?'' asked Pryor.

Egypt shook her head. ''It needs nothing. Girl, you've got beautiful shoulders. And look at that nice long neck.'' She'd added a modicum of makeup to Pryor's face, a bit of lipstick and mascara. ''You look like a fairy princess or the Snow Queen, sugar.''

When there was a knock on the front door, all three jumped. Pryor suddenly felt reluctant, a bit frightened, then she looked again at the vision in the mirror.

"I'll get it," said Egypt. She turned to Pryor. "Don't appear just yet. Wait until he's inside, then make an entrance down the stairs."

Pryor did as she was told, noticing how unbelievably handsome Win was in white tie and tails. She walked slowly, relishing the glow of admiration in his eyes.

As soon as she slipped on the long white cape and pinned Win's orchid to her beaded white purse, the fairy tale began. There was a brief moment when she wondered if Thomas would be there and what he would look like in tails. She repressed the thought.

The hall where the party was held was only a few blocks away. Pryor saw couples in evening clothes going in, heard laughter, the distant sound of music. An attendant took their car and they ascended the steps to the festivities.

After she'd left her cape in the cloakroom, Win led her into the main hall. Flowers were everywhere, draped over the windows, covering a trellis before the stage where the band sat. Wrought-iron candelabra surrounded the room, glowing in the large, barely lit space.

The receiving line was to the left. Mr. and Mrs. Blackshear, portly and beaming, flanked the debutante. Serena Blackshear obviously was a social disaster. Too tall, too thin, she wore a hoop-skirted dress of white taffeta that did nothing for her figure. Her peaked little face was desperate. The glasses and stiff Scarlett O'Hara–type curls did little to help.

There were two bars and two tables of food. People had started dancing. The band was playing something by Cole Porter. Pryor never had seen more beautiful young girls. A bevy of elegant dowagers sat on the sidelines.

After they'd gone through the receiving line, Pryor pressing poor Serena's sweaty little hand, Win took her in his arms, and they moved onto the dance floor. Within seconds a tall young man cut in, smiling down at her. Before she could ask his name, another man, older with a goatee, took over, then another and another. At last she was back in Win's arms. "You're the belle of the ball, Pryor."

"Do you think they see a dollar sign on my forehead?"

"What a little cynic you are! Most of these men don't know who you are. All they see is a beautiful woman."

Someone cut in and then someone else. She

drifted, she soared, letting her mind go blank, blissful in the unreal glory of the moment. At last, exhausted, she excused herself and went to the ladies' room. There were a few giggling girls at the mirrors but they departed quickly. At the farthest mirror, Pryor saw the hoop-skirted person whom the party celebrated. She was mopping her face with a paper towel and apparently had been crying. Pryor moved to her. "Can I help you, Serena?"

A blurred face with lopsided glasses turned to her.

"I wish I was dead." The voice was childlike.

"You're not having a good time?"

"It's horrible. No one really wants to dance with me. I can't dance. I step on their feet, trip on this dress. Mom and Dad said I had to do this, made me come."

"I know how you feel," said Pryor.

Serena looked at Pryor, beautiful in her peach chiffon dress. "No you don't. Everyone wants to dance with you."

"It wasn't always that way. Listen, Serena, at my first dance I was a real klutz, spent all my time in the ladies' room, staring at the bands on my teeth, my freckles. Then, I thought, the heck with it. I flounced out to the dance floor, smiled at everyone, greeted everyone, and found some poor shy boy and asked him to dance with me. I was a sight, but slowly other boys cut in. How I tossed my head, laughed at their jokes.''

''I can't do that.'' She looked at herself in the mirror.

''Here, let me help you.'' Pryor removed the glasses, combed out the stiff curls until they fluffed softly around Serena's face. She added lipstick, a little perfume from her purse. Serena stared at her reflection. She wasn't gorgeous but she could hold her own. She turned and smiled at Pryor. Her lovely, long-lashed eyes glowed. Her smile transformed her face.

''Can you see without your glasses?''

''Enough.'' They both laughed.

They left the ladies' room together, Serena going first. Her shoulders were straight, her head high. Pryor saw Win, motioned to him, discreetly pointed toward Serena. He came at once, bowed slightly, and winged away, Serena in his arms.

Pryor was claimed at once by an elderly man whose hands shook and who counted under his breath as he danced. He immediately was replaced by a handsome, young type who swirled her around the floor while other dancers pulled back to watch. She saw Serena across the room, being cut in on several times. Serena's smile was radiant.

Pryor and Win were among the last to leave. She didn't want it to end, this magic evening when she at last was what she'd dreamed of being. But she was tired and sleepy and her feet hurt. She was glad to be back in Win's car, wrapped in her white cape.

At her door he made no amorous advances. But he looked at her as if to memorize her, took her hand, and kissed her forehead.

Chapter Twelve

Miranda called her the next morning with another invitation. She and Bruce were having a supper party on their boat. "You've got to see the town from the harbor, Pryor. It's quite something."

Pryor accepted with thanks. "Just Linda and Cleve and two couples I think you'll enjoy," said Miranda. "Oh, and Win will be coming." There was a slight pause and then Miranda spoke casually. "I hear you cut quite a swath at the Blackshear party, dancing with every man there. We had to miss it because Bruce had a bad sinus headache."

"It was fun."

After they'd hung up Pryor wondered for the hundredth time whether Miranda disliked her or simply lacked charm. Anyway, she loved the idea of a boat party. She'd never been aboard a boat and she looked forward to seeing the town from the harbor.

I'm having a brisk social life, she thought. *Never in my whole life have I been to so many parties.* She could not forget Rose or the cord across the steps or the brakes of her car, but she desperately wanted some simple, nonthreatening explanation. She wanted to belong here.

As usual, she and Egypt debated about what she was to wear. Egypt opted for a classy white silk pantsuit. Pryor decided to wear her white jeans and the white cashmere sweater.

The day of the party dawned blue and cloudless, not hot but barely cool.

Win called for her about three o'clock. In blue jeans and a navy sweater, he looked unlike himself but happy and relaxed. They parked near the marina and walked down a long dock to where the *Stargazer* was moored.

Pryor was glad they were early because Miranda took her on a tour of the boat. About sixty feet long, painted a bright blue, its big main cabin held the helm and the dashboard as well as long inbuilt seats facing each other.

There were a few deck chairs and a low table. Below was the galley, the head, and another cabin with four berths. Beyond this was another smaller cabin and berth, for the captain, Miranda explained. At the very back of the boat was a canvas-canopied deck with a low railing and a number of deck chairs. Miranda introduced Pryor to Sam Volmer, the captain, a stocky, cigar-smoking man of indeterminate age.

The others arrived shortly. Pryor greeted Linda and Cleve, Charlie and Marge Lytell, and Virginia and Will Hogan. Charlie and Marge could only be described as medium people, medium height, weight, and brown hair. Virginia and Will were a bit more vivid. She was almost beautiful, tall with bright blue eyes and a blond pigtail over one shoulder. Will had a potbelly and thinning hair, rather bulging eyes, and a perpetual smile. Right behind them came Bruce, carrying a big bag of what looked like liquor.

Everyone was in high spirits. There were loud greetings, laughter, an air of festivity. Most of them gathered on the back deck as the captain steered them from the marina. Bruce mixed drinks in the galley as they moved down the Ashley River.

Pryor was amazed at the simple effect of being on the water. The uneasiness and fears of the past weeks faded away. She sipped her drink and observed the town from the harbor. She saw the sidewalked seawall where tourists roamed, the row of gorgeous eighteenth-and nineteenth-century houses facing the water, a skyline with few tall buildings but many church spires.

"What an incredible place to live," said Pryor to no one in particular.

"It is indeed," remarked Bruce from behind her, "and has been since 1670. At first the settlers lived up the Ashley River a way, to escape the Spanish. Later they settled the peninsula."

"Amazing old Charleston," remarked Charlie Lytell to the left of her. "It's survived fire, earthquake, hurricanes, and two enemy occupations, first the British and then the Yankees."

They moved beyond the harbor to open sea, Bruce pointing out Fort Sumter, which wasn't as big as Pryor expected. There were more drinks, and hot hors d'oeuvres which Miranda heated in a microwave oven. Some of the guests sat in the main cabin, others on the afterdeck. It couldn't have been more relaxed. They waved to passing sailboats and powerboats. Bruce played music on his stereo; Will sang in a pleasing baritone. Win chimed in. The others joined him. It wasn't the Mormon choir, but it wasn't half bad.

This is the way life should be, thought Pryor. It was the way hers never had been. She felt part of this group, entitled to such a day.

The beautiful day deepened into dusk. Supper was served in the main cabin, the only well-lit place on the boat. They lined up on the long seats, with some sitting on deck chairs, and ate a delicious chili con carne, broccoli aspic, and French bread. Although they used paper plates, it seemed curiously elegant. After dinner they dispersed, most of them to the afterdeck. Pryor stood by the low railing and stared shoreward.

Suddenly Virginia Hogan, standing to her right, called out, ''It's a dolphin!'' Sure enough, the long silver-gray body was swimming close to the boat. The others left the main cabin and joined them. Pryor was thrilled, leaned further forward to get a good view. She saw it plunge down, then reappear. All the guests were there to see it. They milled about in the darkness. Will Hogan, who'd had quite a bit to drink, fell over a deck chair. Others, no better off, helped him to his feet. ''That darn light's gone,'' said Bruce. ''Forgot to replace it.''

Pryor was aware of the music blaring, a great

deal of talking and laughter. She was good-
naturedly pushed, shoved. She tried to move
away from the rail, but was barricaded. She
tried to be a good sport, sang along with the
others.

Suddenly, the water began to get rough, toss-
ing the boat from side to side. Deck chairs slid
about, people stumbled. The music played on.

Without first realizing, Pryor felt her feet
slipping. Her hands were wrenched from the
railing and she was moving forward, down-
ward. Then her head hit the water, then her
whole body. It was dark and cold. It filled her
eyes, nose, and mouth, pulled her down, down.
She heard the boat move on; the sounds become
less clear. She tried calling out. No one heard.
The music and voices were too loud. She was
numb with panic, realizing that her clothing
was pulling her down. She pushed upward and
for a second grabbed a lungful of air, then she
was going under again. Frantically, she pulled
off her sneakers and then, with difficulty, her
jeans. She managed to surface, gasping but feeling a little lighter. She was able to tread water.
In the distance she saw the *Stargazer* heading
for the harbor. No one had missed her. She was
alone in the dark water. Each of the guests

would assume she was somewhere else on the boat.

She had no idea how long she was treading water, going under from exhaustion and then managing to surface again. She thought of swimming to shore, but knew she couldn't make it. She was almost sure she was to die there in the dark water when she saw in the distance a pale light. A boat! At once she screamed, screamed again. Now there was an incentive to tread water, to hope.

When miraculously it came into sight, she saw that it was a small sailboat, going shoreward under power. She screamed as loudly as she could. The boat picked up speed. She could see two figures, two men—no, they were boys. They turned toward her. She was treading water madly, waving in their direction. Then all of her energy seemed to evaporate and she felt herself going under. The water was claiming her. One last wave, one weak scream and she was sinking, her arm still upraised.

Suddenly she felt an ironlike clasp on her upraised wrist. She reached out her other hand and it too was grabbed tightly. She was being pulled over the side of the boat. She lay there too weak to speak or move. One of the boys took off his jacket and helped her into it. The other got a sandy blanket from the prow and wrapped it around her. They stared at her and she stared back. They looked about eighteen. One had curly red hair and was skinny. The other, a shaggy blond, wore a baseball cap backwards.

It was a small boat, no longer under sail but propelled by a sturdy motor. On the deck were a number of empty soda cans and hamburger wrappers.

"Are you all right?" asked the redhead finally.

"Yes," she managed. "I guess the others didn't realize I'd gone over."

Neither spoke so she added, "The afterdeck light had burned out."

"You're cold," said the one in the baseball cap. He pulled her closer, between his knees, and wrapped his arms around her. "I'm Dirk Patterson and that's Will Burton. Will, go get a blanket."

"I'm Pryor Dimitri."

This seemed to finish the conversation. They proceeded toward the marina.

Pryor, grateful for Dirk Patterson's warm arms holding the blanket snug around her, tried to get her thoughts together. How had this happened to her? What had become of the festive, happy day, her feeling of being part of a group? Of course, the *Stargazer* had been rolling in a rough sea. There was a lot of drinking, pushing, shoving, and tripping over things. It was unfortunate but understandable.

They slid into a slip at the marina. At once Pryor saw the group from the *Stargazer* milling around, talking to three policemen. She saw an ambulance on shore, parked near the water. The boys helped her out of the boat and she stood on the dock, still dripping wet, wearing Dirk's jacket, her long, soaked sweater reaching to her knees.

''That's my group,'' she told Dirk and Will.

With one on either side of her, they picked their way to the *Stargazer* party. One by one the party discovered her, crying out with amazement and relief. It was Win who reached her first, grabbing her in his arms as if he'd never let her go. She could feel his heart beating.

''Oh, Pryor! Thank goodness you're all right. We all thought—we couldn't find you—it was horrible!'' He held her even closer.

The others flocked around. Linda and even Miranda had been crying. They exclaimed, thanked heaven, and touched her with concern.

"Win," she finally whispered, "take me home, please."

She thanked Dirk and Will, finding words inadequate; gave Dirk his jacket. Win led her to his car, carrying her across the parking lot to protect her bare feet. It took only a few minutes to reach the house on Tradd Street. Win had been silent and she knew it was from relief. When he helped her from the car, he was pale and his body shaking.

He didn't use his key but knocked on the big door. It opened almost at once. For a few seconds Egypt regarded them with some astonishment and then pulled Pryor inside. Win left at once. Egypt stood back, taking in Pryor's wet hair and soaked sweater.

"Was it a good party?" she asked casually.

"Egypt, let me explain—"

Egypt again observed the clinging wet sweater and the long bare legs. "Sweetie," she said, "I never question what my friends do."

Chapter Thirteen

Egypt did not question her that night. She helped her into a warm bath, dried her off, slipped one of the beautiful nightgowns over her head, and tucked her in bed. She touched her hand gently. "I'm right next door if you need me."

The next morning when Sylvia, followed by Egypt, brought her breakfast tray, she asked them to sit. She told them in detail what had happened on the boat, how she had lost her balance, no one realizing she was gone because of the dark, of being picked up by the boys in the sailboat.

There was a considerable silence and then

quite suddenly a loud knocking on the front door. They all started with surprise.

"I'll get it." Sylvia hurried from the room.

Egypt and Pryor looked at each other. Pryor looked away first. "You don't believe me, Egypt."

"Oh, I believe you." She paused. "You don't remember being pushed?"

"There was a lot of pushing and shoving. I told you that."

"What next?" asked Egypt.

Pryor thought carefully. "I shall proceed as if I've had an accident."

"Like the cord across the steps and the car wreck?"

"Yes."

"You are one crazy lady, Pryor!"

"I guess so."

Thomas rushed into the room without knocking, came to the side of the bed, and looked at Pryor intently.

"Hello," she said.

"I just had to see that you're all right."

"I'm fine. How did you know? No, don't tell me. Sylvia told Bubber's cook, she told Bubber, and he told you. The Charleston network."

"Yes. And we're particularly fascinated by coincidences."

''Thomas, aren't you going to grab me in your arms and cover me with kisses?'' She grinned.

''No.'' He walked to the window, looked out at the rather murky day. ''Pryor, I've been wanting to talk to you.''

''Talk now.'' Her eyes softened as she looked at the tall figure, barefoot and in worn shorts, one dark curl falling over his forehead.

''I think you should leave Charleston.''

Her heart missed a beat. ''How do you mean?''

''I mean don't stay because of our relationship. I mean I hope you'll take your inheritance and get out of Charleston.''

''I see.''

''I'm afraid for you. Can you understand that?''

''Yes.''

''Will you forgive me?'' It was almost a whisper.

She yearned toward him. ''Yes.''

''I want you to have a good life, everything you've always wanted.'' He turned to her, his eyes so full of love it was more than she could bear.

He left the room so quickly she couldn't reply.

It was a day of callers. She didn't see most of them but they left gifts of flowers, candy, casseroles, and all manner of delicacies. Sylvia was ecstatic as the food accumulated. Pryor was glad she had time to recover from her scene with Thomas before the family arrived. Miranda, Bruce, Linda, and Cleve entered the room almost timidly. Win came last, not timidly but apologetically. As if on cue came the exclamations.

"Oh Pryor, thank heaven you're safe!"

"We can't believe it really happened."

"Of course, we all were drinking too much."

"Yes. And the lack of light."

"Are you sure you're all right?"

Miranda had brought a pie, Linda brownies, and the men flowers.

"Listen," she addressed them all, "I'm fine. I appreciate your concern." She settled back on the pillows, feeling she had the upper hand. "I'm glad you've all come. There's something I wanted to talk to you about."

"You've more leads about Rosie's death?" Bruce spoke abruptly.

Pryor wished she'd asked Thomas if he'd discovered anything about the tampering with Althea's investment, the deposit in someone's savings account. "I expect to hear any minute."

"Can't you share it with us?" Despite the cool day Cleve was sweating.

"Not yet, but I will soon. I wanted to talk to you about something else. Althea's estate. I've never felt right about it. So I've made a decision. We're going to share it."

There was total silence, amazed faces.

Pryor went on. "All I want is enough to buy a small house on a creek somewhere and to buy a car. Besides that I'll need investment money to bring a modest income. The rest and the house and everything in it is yours." She looked at Miranda and Linda. "That should bring you over a million apiece."

Linda burst into tears. Miranda turned pale, came to Pryor, took her hand. "That," she said, "is the most generous thing I've ever heard of."

"Part of it's selfish," said Pryor. "I'm hoping that I'll feel safer, freer."

Win Hazzard spoke. "Pryor, are you sure you want to do this? It's quite a step."

"In the right direction I hope, Win. I'd like you to draw up the proper papers."

He walked to the window, glanced at the garden. "If it's what you want."

There was more to be said but no one seemed capable of putting it into words. Miranda came to the bed, put her arms around Pryor, kissed her. Linda did the same, managing to drop her purse, her Kleenex, and get Pryor's cheek wet. All looked at Pryor in astonishment.

"Now," said Pryor, "if you'll forgive me, I'd like to take a short nap. Miranda, thank you for the pecan pie; Linda, bless you for the brownies. As for you gentlemen, I'm thrilled with the flowers."

They left the room quietly. She watched them go. As soon as they'd left Egypt entered. "What kind of shot did you give them?" she asked. "They look like it's Christmas morning."

When Pryor told her what she proposed to do, Egypt raised both eyebrows, shook her head. "In danger of repeating myself, may I say that you are one crazy lady."

Instead of dreaming about drowning, Pryor dreamed that she was ten years old and trying to find the exit to Disneyland.

At nine o'clock the next morning she called the real estate man suggested by Egypt. He was enchanted and turned up within the hour. A small, meager man, he had thinning black hair, pointed features, and small pointed shoes. The creases of Henry Bremer's trousers could have cut bread and his Cadillac was worthy of a Mafia boss.

It was a beautiful, cloudless day and Pryor got quite a tour of the Low Country. They looked at countless properties, went through houses of brick, cinderblock, and frame. Some of them were attractive but none really grabbed her. "I'm afraid," said Henry Bremer, "that's about it." He was turning the car around to leave the last prospect, a hacienda-type dwelling, when he slowed, looked at her dubiously. "Of course there is one other."

"It's getting late," said Pryor despondently. Then she asked, "What's wrong with it?"

Henry actually blushed, considered lying, then blurted out the truth. "I've been trying to get the owner to put a higher price on it. He refuses. He's a weird old coot, a stickler for what he thinks of as fairness."

"Let's go," said Pryor.

For the next half hour they went down a highway and then what seemed an endless dirt road. At the end of this they drew up beside a one-story cypress building. It was so unobtrusive it seemed part of the trees and shrubs around it. The gray slate roof and stone chimney matched the unpainted cypress. Just beyond it was a creek with a dock and a wide expanse of marsh stretching for miles. Pryor caught her breath. "Can we look inside?"

"Of course. I have a key here somewhere."

They approached the big front door, painted azure and the only spot of color in the soft grayness of the house. Once inside, Pryor looked around in wonder. They'd entered a sizeable living room, leading to what seemed a well-equipped kitchen. She looked at a copper chandelier, deep-set windows, some with seats below, a huge stone fireplace, wide polished floorboards. Henry led her through four smallish bedrooms and two attractive baths. When they stood again in the living room Pryor took a long breath.

"I'll take it," she said.

"Are you sure?"

"Today. Now. Before you get the owner to double the price."

When they stepped again into the outdoors, the sun was setting beyond the marsh, which was bathed in a rose-gold. Pryor saw a heron, a wood stork, an egret. Just beyond the house was a small, vine-covered gazebo and beyond that two huge magnolia trees and a number of moss-hung live oaks. In the morning one could sit on the dock, drink a cup of coffee, and watch the world come awake. In the evening one could sit in the gazebo, sip a drink, and watch the sun make a watercolor of the marsh.

She had time to think on the way home. Henry was not much given to conversation. She came to two conclusions. Thomas was not about to become involved with her. The second conclusion was that the attempts on her life had nothing to do with money. Someone was afraid she knew too much about Rose's death, but she would not stop in her determination to uncover more. For years it was assumed that Rose had left town; now Pryor had opened a Pandora's box and the murderer was trying to get rid of her. This both frightened her and made her more stubborn. She'd have to talk to Thomas, see what he had found out about withdrawals and deposits.

She thought of Thomas with longing, tried to put him out of her mind, failed. Like so many of the things she wanted in life, he was beyond her.

Henry Bremer drew up in front of her house. He said they'd complete the negotiations for the property the next day after he'd consulted the owner. She agreed, left the car, unlocked the big front door, and entered. Persis was waiting for her but pretended she just happened to be resting in the hall. Pryor heard Egypt and Sylvia's voices coming from the kitchen, petted the cat, and went to greet the two women, who were cutting up vegetables and having a mild argument.

Egypt greeted her from the sink. "Well! Any luck?"

Pryor sat at the table, slipped off her shoes. "All kinds of luck."

Sylvia poured three cups of coffee and they all gathered at the table. "Tell us about it, darlin'."

She did, describing the house, the grounds, the view, the modest price. Her enthusiasm was catching. All of them were smiling. Egypt made no cryptic remarks. Sylvia beamed and declared, "Things are gonna change for you now. I feel it in my bones."

Chapter Fourteen

In the next few days Pryor thought often of Sylvia's statement that things were going to change for her. In a way, they did. There were no more catastrophes. Life smoothed out. She was certain that Miranda's intervention prompted invitations for her to join St. Michael's church, the Junior League, and the DAR, all of which she declined. She made contributions to the Crisis Center, the SPCA, and the Friends of Old Charleston. She took long walks on the Battery.

She took Sylvia and Egypt to see her house on the creek the same day she acquired ownership. They loved it, especially when she assured Sylvia that she would still require her services. When she showed it to Miranda and Linda they were just as enthusiastic.

"You're sure you don't want the Tradd Street house?" asked Linda.

"No. It's not my style. The minute I saw this house I had to have it."

"It's a treasure," agreed Miranda.

Pryor had seen the two sisters eying the various furnishings of Althea's house and suggested that they take turns in making their selections. The next day they did, Miranda choosing the most valuable antiques and Linda opting for what she considered "the prettiest." They would pick them up as soon as Pryor moved.

Pryor went to a family dinner at Miranda's, just the five of them and Win Hazzard. After an especially fine meal, they sat in the drawing room and enjoyed liqueurs. Once more they talked about family history, mostly of General Elias Amory who fought the British in 1778 and entitled the girls to membership in the DAR. Miranda rose from the sofa, went to a desk, and returned with a dark blue velvet box, which she handed to Pryor. Inside Pryor found a gold necklace with a medallion.

"It's the family seal," explained Miranda,

"given to me by my grandmother. That seal goes back, oh, I don't know—"

"To the Battle of Hastings," suggested Linda.

"Yes."

Pryor touched the medallion; tears rose in her eyes. "How very kind of you."

It was again Bruce who brought up the subject of Rose. "Have you got any more leads?" he asked casually.

Pryor was silent for a few seconds. She wished she had heard from Thomas. She longed just to hear his voice. "I think I'm getting close," she said with what she hoped was conviction.

Win offered to drive Pryor home but she assured him she hadn't walked, but had driven her newly repaired car. He followed her to make sure she arrived safely.

She invited Bubber Perrigeau to supper and he accepted with enthusiasm. He arrived promptly, wearing his red vest, a dark blue blazer, and a bow tie. His mop of curly white hair was carefully combed and he presented Pryor with a gift. When Pryor unwrapped it she found a dark-green bottle.

"Early eighteenth century," said Bubber proudly.

He insisted that they dine in the kitchen and that Egypt and Sylvia join them. It was a festive meal—okra gumbo, country ham, grits, turnip greens, and corn bread. They laughed a lot. Bubber and Sylvia reminisced about the old days, the people they'd known. Bubber told Pryor about Sam Stoney, Milby Burton, Alfred Hutty, and DuBose Heyward. Sylvia remembered Beth Verner, Maud Waddell, and Josephine Pinckney.

''And of course,'' said Bubber, ''there was Rosie. We've never had another like Rosie.''

''Tell me about her,'' urged Pryor.

''Well, to begin with, she was beautiful.'' Bubber's eyes were misty. ''But that was of no concern to her except that she found it amusing so many men were in love with her. She was fascinated by life and by people, what made them tick. She knew more about this town than anyone. Rosie. Mysteries drove her crazy. She'd prod and nose around until she found the truth. Old Reneé Gaston was the worst possible snob, insisted her ancestors were French nobility. Rosie discovered that her great-great-great-grandfather was a butcher in Nantes. She also uncovered the fact that the town meanie, Lorraine Prynne, had an illegitimate grandmother who was part Native American.'' Bubber laughed heartily. ''That was our Rosie. There were no secrets from her.''

Pryor was fascinated. She couldn't stop herself. ''Bubber, do you think it was something she discovered that led to her death?''

''She used to play chess with me every Thursday night. Led to her death? Who knows? Rose was full of surprises.'' Pryor noticed that there were tears in his eyes.

He thanked them for the dinner, told them that Thomas was in Washington and that he'd been lonely.

As he was leaving, he held Pryor's face between his hands. ''Bless you, dear.'' Then his voice took on a serious note. ''And take care. Yes, take care.''

The next day Pryor, aided by Sylvia and Egypt, set out to furnish the river house. She bought a long sofa covered with batik and matching armchairs, side tables, lamps, a pine coffee table, a handsome desk, and an occasional chair. She equipped the bedrooms with brass beds, plain bureaus, and antique rocking chairs. The kitchen needed only dishes, flatware, glasses, a few pots and pans. All in all, the house was ready to welcome its owner. She decided to avoid curtains because of the view, and to buy paintings slowly and carefully. Furnished, the house was a godsend. It drew her mind away from the terror of the past weeks. She was lulled not into complacency but a strong sense of hope.

Miranda and Linda had decided to sell Althea's house. Neither wanted to live there. The memory of Rose, buried in the garden, left too terrible a residue. Miranda worried about the hole near the piazza, now abandoned by the police. Pryor assured her that Thomas undoubtedly would plant the magnolia, lying alongside, its roots covered with a length of damp burlap. Very soon the place would be ready to show to prospective buyers.

Pryor began to make allowances for Miranda's and Linda's faults, to like them for the good in them. She stopped feeling that their warmth toward her was due to her generosity. Both gave her large, arching green plants for her new house. Both called her each day to see if they could be of some help.

Finally, Thomas called. He was in Washington and in his own words was onto something. Like Bubber, he urged her to take care.

"Under no circumstances," he said, "should you stay in that house alone." Except for that, there was nothing personal in his call. It was all just the business at hand. How she longed for a note of affection.

Miranda and Bruce took her to hear the symphony, which was excellent. Linda and Cleve took her to a play at the Footlight Players, which she enjoyed. Bubber took her to a fish fry on Edisto Island and despite the mosquitoes she had a good time.

She found some large suitcases in the attic and she and Egypt packed her stylish clothes and some books. At last she was ready to move to the house on the river.

''I'll spend a few days with you there,'' said Egypt. ''I've got a little of my vacation left.''

She knew she was beginning a new life.

Chapter Fifteen

She awoke two mornings later not only to brilliant sunlight, but to the sight of a long white envelope on her bedside table. At first she thought it was another letter from Evelyn. However, the envelope had no name and no stamp. When she opened it she found an airline ticket, passage to Atlanta, and then to Paris, France. She stared at it, mouth agape with surprise. She had not yet closed her mouth when there was a tap on the door and Egypt entered.

"Well," she said, sitting on the side of the bed, "you game?"

"You crazy, Egypt?"

"It's time to blow town, sugar, have a

change of scene. Haven't you always wanted to see Paris?''

''Yes, but . . .''

''No buts. I've made hotel reservations already. I'm going with you. We'll share the costs. Like a little lamb, you need protection. All set.''

Pryor sat staring at her. ''My new house, Egypt,'' she began.

''It's all furnished and the papers are signed. Sylvia will keep an eye on things here. I'm sure Bubber will see to the place in the country and Win can handle the passports.''

''But these tickets are for the day after tomorrow.''

''How long does it take to pack?''

Every objection was met with a reasonable answer from Egypt. Actually Pryor found that she desperately wanted to go. She called Miranda, Linda, Bubber, and Win to tell them of her plans. Instead of being stunned, they all were delighted for her.

''It's just what you need,'' said Miranda. ''You've not had an easy time since you got here.''

''Be sure you see Saint Chapelle,'' advised Bubber. ''It's an experience.''

There was no way to tell Thomas since he was out of town on an assignment.

"Somewhere in the Mideast," mused Bubber. "I'm not quite sure where."

When she called Evelyn, she was greeted not by cynicism, but cries of ecstasy. Evelyn felt that Pryor's life had truly turned into a fairy tale. "And listen," said Pryor, "I'm sending you some money to take that trip out west you always wanted. You can find your own John Wayne." Evelyn didn't refuse. She hiccoughed and then burst into tears.

Helped by Egypt and Sylvia, Pryor packed one of Aunt Althea's beautiful big Vuitton bags.

Before she knew it, she and Egypt were on a plane to Atlanta, had arrived in that enormous city, and were sitting in the VIP lounge. When it came time to board the plane to Paris, Pryor felt nothing beyond a sense of unreality. Everything was first class—the seats, the food, the attentions of the French stewardess. It turned out that Egypt had friends in Paris, old chums from law school she intended to contact.

Pryor slept during most of the trip to Paris, declining drinks and dinner. She dreamed of Mark Whiteside. When Egypt shook her and announced that they were approaching Orly Airport outside Paris, she was vastly relieved.

She stepped into an unfamiliar world, where everyone was well dressed and jibbered in a strange language. They rented a small Renault, packed in their luggage, and set out for the dream city.

Pryor was now wide awake but already in a state of bedazzlement. Every mile seemed redolent with history. She thought of Marie Antoinette being driven in her gorgeous carriage, of Napoleon setting out with his army. A sense of unreality persisted.

The unreality was enhanced by the city itself, the boulevards in contrast to the narrow streets, the storied Seine River. It was further enhanced by their lodging, a small hotel converted from a seventeenth-century house.

''The big, snappy hotels are dazzling,'' said Egypt, ''but they're not the real Paris.''

They had two rooms with a wall of French doors and a shared balcony. The furniture was French Provincial. The bathroom had a black-and-white tiled floor and a simply enormous tub.

They had dinner in the basement restaurant, snails in a delicious sauce and an unforgettable steak with *pommes frites.* After dinner they simply walked, entranced by the lights of Paris, by the sights and sounds. They had cappuccinos at a sidewalk café and brandy in a dusky boîte. They walked until they were ready to drop. Finally, Egypt suggested bed and they returned to their hotel. Before she slept Pryor sat on a window seat, staring at the glittering city. She wondered if Paris ever slept.

The next morning a flood of sunlight awoke her. It gilded the room. She and Egypt had croissants and coffee on the balcony. Both dressed in smart wool suits, they set out to further inspect the city. Pryor was reminded of all the books she'd read with a French setting, the colorful history of Paris. She was moved to tears in the glory of Notre Dame, the Paris Opera House, the Louvre. She saw sights she never would forget. She saw why the poet had written *"Paris is a woman's town, with flowers in her hair."*

She saw Thomas.

He was sitting at an outdoor café drinking coffee and reading *The New York Times*. He wore a gray suit and his curly dark hair was windblown. Egypt marched up to him at once. Then he was on his feet, viewing them first with what seemed consternation, then with joy. He hugged them each.

''I don't know what to say,'' he mumbled. ''I'm amazed, startled, and taken aback.''

He made room for them at his table. There in the setting sun they drank Camparis and talked of Paris. Thomas invited them to go with him that night to the opera.

''It's *La Bohême,*'' he said. ''We can all have a good cry and admire the Paris Opera.''

The only one who cried was Pryor, deeply touched by the opera and the gorgeous surroundings. She still couldn't believe what had happened, that she was sitting beside Thomas. She warned herself of her own naïveté, reminded herself of the episode with Mark Whiteside. She was sure that Thomas, like the men she'd known, was not only adept at flirting but backing off. He was not a man to make a commitment.

But when he said good night at the door of the fine old house, he made her promise to meet him in the morning. Egypt would be seeing friends and he wanted to show her the town.

She thought a lot about Thomas before she slept. He seemed to devour her with his eyes but his demeanor was that of a friend. The next day they were entranced by the splendor of Notre Dame, marveled at the exquisite little Saint Chapelle. They went to endless galleries, large and small. They even walked by the Seine; at night watched the boats, the lights of the city. Through all of this, Thomas seemed cautious, courtly, informative but with all the ardor of a tour guide.

Later she couldn't remember when it was that he suggested that they go to England for a weekend.

"We're so close," he said. "Egypt is off to Provence to see more friends. Please come."

She could tell by the look on his face that it was important to him.

"I have friends in the country," he went on, "who would love to have us come for a visit. Lord Winship. You've got to see the English countryside."

She didn't recall saying yes, only the glow on her friend's face. "Perfect," said Egypt. "It is awfully close. Pierre and Aimee would welcome you to Provence but this is too good to pass up. Good old Thomas!"

Pryor was dazzled by the idea of a weekend at the country estate of an English lord. She also was a bit daunted. She'd heard that the English upper class was cold, snobbish, and thought little of Americans. But it was a chance to see something she'd read much about, a chance to be with Thomas.

The flight to Heathrow seemed to take no more than minutes. Thomas rented a car and drove into London. They didn't stop, but he pointed out Buckingham Palace, Westminster Abbey, St. Paul's Cathedral, and the Houses of Parliament. They lunched at Rule's where Pryor recognized several stage stars. Thomas was even more courtly, more solicitous, kindly, but never intimate.

Then they drove out of the city and Pryor was enchanted to see a sparkling stream where an old man fished and a small boy watched. Across hills she saw stately mansions. It was as green as she imagined Ireland would be.

"Rain." Thomas laughed. "A little bit each day."

She didn't drowse, lest she miss something. She stared at the landscape, at Thomas's strong yet sensitive hands on the wheel, at his imposing profile. With his unruly hair and delighted smile, she easily could picture him as ten years old.

They moved onto a narrower road, flanked by hedgerows. An occasional herd of sheep slowed them down. Elderly men, in plus fours and with dogs, were out taking walks.

The sky cleared; the slight mist of rain ceased. They were climbing a low hill and suddenly there were no more hedgerows. There was a curved driveway leading to a gray stone Georgian mansion.

They left the car next to the steps leading to the huge front door. Thomas barely touched the knocker before the door swung open. An elderly man in butler's garb stood before them.

"Mr. Thomas!" he exclaimed, his face aglow. "Oh, Mr. Thomas!" He was about to embrace Thomas when he remembered his place. "His Lordship is in the library, waiting for you."

"Thank you, Hodge." Thomas patted his shoulder. "This is Miss Dimitri."

Pryor noticed a liveried footman cross the marble-floored hall. Directly beyond was a curved stairway. The walls were hung with ancient portraits.

She was unprepared for Lord Harold Winship. He was the most elegant man she'd ever seen or imagined. His thick dark hair was streaked with silver, his face worthy of a Roman coin. When he stood she realized how tall he was, how innately graceful. His smile warmed the rather cool room.

"Dear boy," he murmured in a deep voice. He embraced Thomas, then turned to Pryor.

"Welcome, Miss Dimitri. You are most welcome."

Pryor was to remember little of what followed. She remembered sitting on a deep leather sofa with Thomas, the drinks, the glowing fire. Then she remembered ascending the curved stairway, being led by Hodge to a peach and silver room where an Irish maid whose cheeks were rosy and speech heavily accented helped her to unpack. She was grateful for the clothes Althea had provided. After a bath in a blue marble tub, she dressed in a long-sleeved, high-necked emerald-green dress, adding a simple but authentic gold necklace.

She thought of Charleston, her relatives, the inheritance, the bones in the garden, of Overton. She thought of what only could be attempts on her life. They were far away, in another world. She brushed her hair until it shone. She went down to dinner.

The meal was interrupted by a great deal of laughter from Thomas and Lord Winship. Pryor sat to the left of Lady Winship, a beautiful middle-aged woman in a wheelchair. They dined, in what Thomas whispered to her was the family's room. The food was perfect, including roast beef and Yorkshire pudding.

Pryor felt as if she'd been dropped into a Jane Austen novel.

Lady Winship was charm itself. She was simply dressed, her gray-blond hair drawn into a chignon, her deep blue eyes full of welcome. She was interested without seeming curious. She asked Pryor about Charleston, how she had met Thomas, her interests. There was no talk of lineage or background. Pryor found herself conversing easily, happily. She was told that Lady Winship's lameness was due to a fall from a horse; that she still managed to be an avid gardener; that, sadly, they had no children. The diamond on Lady Winship's finger was the biggest Pryor ever had seen.

During the next few days Pryor's bedazzlement continued. She, Thomas, and Lord Winship rode horseback, fished for trout, played tennis, and, at night, conversed before the fire in the library. Once again Pryor noticed that Thomas was courteous but detached. She could tell he wanted her to have a good time but he evaded involvement.

Pryor realized by now that she loved Thomas deeply. She saw that what she had felt for Mark Whiteside was part of growing up, coming of age, forgivable. What she felt for Thomas went much deeper. She was physically attracted but a great deal more. He was lodged in her heart. She decided she was not lodged in his.

Their last night at Winship Hall was a time of revelation. Lady Winship, resting in her room, had requested that Thomas come and talk to her. They were good friends and she looked forward to some time alone with him.

Pryor sat with Lord Winship in the library as they drank brandies and stared at the fire. She wondered what they would talk about.

"Thomas certainly loves being here," she ventured.

"He's been coming since he was a small boy."

"I see. His parents were your friends?"

There was a pause and then a rueful laugh. "You might say so."

It was an odd answer and Pryor looked at him closely.

The question from Lord Winship was sudden, an unexpected non sequitur. "Are you in love with Thomas?"

She was taken aback. She couldn't deny it, but she hesitated to reveal herself. "Why do you ask?"

"You're the first woman he's ever brought here."

"Yes."

"I thought so."

"But the love is not returned."

"I believe that it is. I can tell by the way that he looks at you." It was spoken gently.

The next remark was also odd. "Treat him kindly," said Lord Winship.

"You're very concerned for him." She longed to get up and run from the room.

The look on his face was one of sadness and also of pride. He seemed to stop and consider what he was about to say. "I loved his mother. He should have been my son."

She said nothing, simply stared at the fire.

He hesitated, took a sip of brandy, and continued. "Only one other person knows—his uncle." She could tell that it was painful for him to speak.

"And his mother?"

"A Charleston girl here on a European tour, following college. We both were very young. We met at a ball in London, loved each other at once."

"Why didn't you marry?"

"It already was arranged that I marry Elaine. In my class, that's the way things are done." It was said quite matter-of-factly, but his eyes told another story.

"You still love her? Thomas's mother?"

He looked away, toward the darkened windows. ''Yes. She married a charming and penniless drifter on the rebound, and less than two years later he killed them both driving home drunk from a party. Her parents were dead, and his would have nothing to do with the baby. Thomas's uncle took him in, brought him up, gave him his name.''

It explained so much about Thomas's aloofness, and she could see by Lord Winship's expression that he hoped she understood.

''No real family,'' he said.

''But—''

He laughed, a low, bitter sound. ''Strange. This whole thing might have been so very different. Our Thomas should have been born here.''

She felt as if her heart would break, thinking of Thomas's lonely childhood. She longed to tell Thomas that she understood, that his mother's sad story was tragic.

She never had the chance. She met Thomas in the vast hall, after saying good night to Lord Winship. His mind already was elsewhere. ''You must forgive me, Pryor, if I don't drive you back to town, to the airport. I've been sent on assignment to Cairo and must leave at once. The family chauffeur will get you to London.

This is a chance I can't pass up.'' For a brief moment his face was ardent. "I'll miss you, Pryor.''

She managed to speak airily. "Don't give it a thought.''

She went to bed in the peach and silver room and managed to sleep dreamlessly. When she went down to breakfast the next morning Thomas already had gone. In keeping with the situation the day was cold and overcast. When the time came for her to go, her good-byes to the Winships were brief and heartfelt. Lord Winship held her in a warm embrace. Lady Winship pulled her down, kissed her, and murmured, "Have a good life, my dear.'' Pryor climbed into a long Mercedes and Cyril drove her to the airport.

She napped on the trip to France, took a taxi at Orly, and was driven to her hotel in Paris. Egypt already waited for her. She reported that her stay in Provence was perfect and waited for Pryor's report. Pryor found herself jabbering mindlessly about the warmth of the Winships, the glamorous house, the horseback riding, fishing, the fabulous gardens. She never mentioned Thomas. Egypt listened, her dark eyes wide. They had their last Paris dinner at the famous Tour d'Argent, packed, and went to bed.

The next morning, their plane to the States took off early. Pryor left Paris as if leaving a dream. She was returning to Charleston with all its problems. She didn't allow herself to think of Thomas. She knew that she must find out what happened to Rose.

She was pleased that she recognized the steeples of St. Philip's and St. Michael's churches and knew she was home. She decided to spend the night in town and go out to the river house in the morning. Miranda and Linda were at the airport to meet them. As she had with Egypt, Pryor jabbered about what she'd seen on her trip and they didn't seem to mind. They listened with great interest.

Sylvia prepared a splendid meal for them. The men appeared and Pryor looked at all of them as they sat at the table, thinking, *We've actually become friends.*

Chapter Sixteen

She lay awake for a long time, thinking of all the things that had happened to her, the promise of the river house. There was a full moon. She watched its glow streaming through the French doors of her bedroom. She couldn't help thinking of Thomas. She wondered if one day she'd give in and marry a Charleston lawyer or doctor, join clubs, do petit point, enjoy gossip, give numbing dinner parties. Or if she might return to Overton, marry a salesman or a claims adjuster, enter her mince preserves in the county fair, discuss detergents over a back fence, and sing in the choir. She prayed she'd do neither.

She wondered if Egypt in the room next door

was asleep and decided that she probably was. Egypt always was in control. If she commanded herself to sleep, she slept. How grateful she was for Egypt's friendship. She admired not only her elegance but her warmth, sense of humor, and keen mind. Thinking of her friend, she finally drifted into sleep.

It must have been an hour later when the phone rang in the upstairs hall. It startled her awake. She pushed back the covers, swung her legs over the side of the bed, and hurried to the hall. Egypt was ahead of her. She could hear her voice, odd, shaky, urgent. ''Is there anyone with her? You say it's a heart attack or a stroke? Oh, no! Look, call EMS right away. Right now! I'll be there as fast as possible.''

Pryor heard the click of the receiver. Bewildered, she saw Egypt's face. She looked haggard, almost old. ''Pryor,'' she said, ''it's my mother. She's sick, bad sick. That was a neighbor, someone Ma managed to call. She abhors doctors. I've got to go. I hate leaving you but I've got to go. I'm Ma's only close family. I've got to be with her.'' She ran back to her room, Pryor following.

''Of course you have to go. Right away. Do you want me to drive you?''

''No.'' Egypt was throwing on clothes, a

shirt, pants, shoes. Then she was facing Pryor. "This is something I have to do myself, Pryor." At the door to the hall, she turned. "Are you sure you'll be all right? I hate to leave you."

"Egypt, go. Don't worry about me. I'll be fine. Oh, darling, I wish there was some way I could help."

"Just pray," said Egypt. "Pray." Then she was gone.

Pryor followed her downstairs and locked the front door after her. Sickened with worry for Sylvia she went back upstairs. Miserable, she crawled back into bed. She tossed and turned and at last, exhausted, fell into a deep, encompassing sleep.

She dreamed she was back in Overton, living in a dreary little house, discussing floor wax with a neighbor, complaining about heavy wax buildup. Then she was in a Charleston drawing room, pouring tea for a dignified dowager and appalling her with a yawn.

Suddenly she was having trouble breathing. *I'm dreaming of drowning,* she thought. *I'm dreaming of the water filling my nose and mouth. I'm going down, down.* But she wasn't. There was no water, just an absence of oxygen, pressure on her head. She felt the softness of the pillow, cutting off air. She struggled, tried to push away the pillow, but it came down hard on her head. Fully awake now, she tried to cry out but the cry was muffled. *I'm being smothered!* she thought wildly. *I'm going to die!* With a great wrench she pulled her head free, scrambled to the other side of the bed, felt her feet touch the floor. Something like a snarl came from opposite her. She looked into a face. The gray-blond hair gleamed in the moonlight, made the features sharper, whiter. The eyes burned at her; the mouth was drawn in a slit. He was around the end of the bed in a flash, reaching for her, almost catching her, but she got to her door, flung it open and raced into the hall. He was close behind her. She could hear the rasping breath. With the barest glance at the steps, she lifted her body to the bannister and she was flying down. There was no newel and she landed with a jolt. Realizing there was not time to unlock the front door she fled to the drawing room, slid behind the nearest drape. He was in the room. He was searching behind sofa, chairs, under the desk. Then he was looking behind drapes, first the ones at the far end of the room, then at the windows facing the piazza. She slipped out, ran across the hall to the dining room. As she passed the fireplace, she grabbed a poker. He was just behind her as she ran around the table, unlocked a French door, and flew outside. As she reached the stairs to the garden, he grabbed her arm. Wildly she swung the poker. It caught him on the shoulder, relaxed his hold, not much but enough for her to pull away and dash down the steps.

"Thomas!" she screamed, but the windows next door were dark. "Thomas!" She ran to the back of the garden, almost brilliant in the moonlight. She crouched behind a bush, still clutching the poker. Win walked slowly, carefully, knowing he'd find her. He'd picked up a shovel and carried it like a rifle. Then at last he saw her, cornered her. He was very close. She lifted the poker to strike him but as she did the shovel came down on the side of her head. First there was excruciating pain and then darkness.

She was not aware of being carried the length of the garden, nor of being thrown in the gaping hole. The first thing she sensed was the dampness, the dirt in her eyes and mouth, more dirt coming from above. Then she knew. She was in Rosie's grave. She was being buried alive.

Being careful not to alert him, Pryor brushed the dirt from her face, tried to breathe easier, to think. He couldn't bury her too deeply. The hole had to look as it always did, with room for the tree to be planted. Somewhere a car door slammed. She could wait until he'd finished and then dig her way upward. An earthworm crawled on her neck and she shuddered, brushed it away. He must have seen because he stopped, stared down. Looking upward she saw him pull out a gun. He was pointing it at her, then a shadow grabbed him from behind. She was aware of a struggle just above her, the sound of falling, then silence.

A coat was being lowered, a dark coat. At once she recognized the voice. ''Pryor, grab this and I'll pull you up. I'd come down but I'm afraid of stepping on you.'' Her hands felt weak but she managed to clutch the coat. Slowly she found herself being drawn upward. When she came to the top of the hole hands reached out and held her. She was pulled upright, barely able to stand. Then she saw Egypt coming through the iron gates to the garden. She saw Win Hazzard lying unconscious.

''Egypt, call the police! And get something to tie his hands,'' called Thomas.

Egypt said nothing but raced to the house, running through the French door that Pryor had left open.

At first, Thomas said nothing, but as he held her close, she could feel the rapid beating of his heart. "Thank goodness you're safe," he murmured. "Thank goodness."

He brushed off most of the dirt, carried her into the house, and put her on the drawing room sofa.

"How did you know?" she asked in a small voice.

"As I was getting out of the taxi I saw him shoveling. With what I knew, I could reach only one conclusion."

Egypt came in with a pale blue shawl which she wrapped around Pryor, then she sat next to her, holding her hand.

"What do you know?" asked Pryor.

Thomas sat in a chair near the sofa. "I know that Win Hazzard had been dipping into your aunt's account for some time. The withdrawals from her investment coincided exactly with deposits in Win's savings account. I'm sure we'll find Rose's diamond necklace and bracelet in his safety-deposit box."

"I can't believe it." Pryor drew the blue afghan closer around her.

"Sugar," said Egypt, "you're always going to look for the good in people, no matter what. Incidentally, I tied Win's hands with the cord from the stairs."

The sound of police sirens invaded the night.

The men trooped into the house, some going into the garden. After a few words with Thomas they were putting handcuffs on Win and leading him to a police car. A nice sergeant sat with Pryor and asked her some questions. Thomas, sitting nearby, told what he had discovered. Egypt reported that she had gotten a false call about her mother and that when she arrived at Sylvia's the old lady was sleeping soundly.

They seemed to be there for hours, asking questions, going through the house and garden. At last they took their leave, after requesting that Pryor come by the precinct house in the morning. Egypt assured them that she would. She all but pushed them out the door before she closed it. She, Thomas, and Pryor stood looking at each other.

''Baby, you look ready to drop.'' Egypt put an arm around Pryor. She looked at Thomas. ''It's time for even heroes to get some sleep.''

''Yes.'' Thomas winked at her and was halfway out the front door before Pryor realized what was happening. She ran after him. He was at the bottom of the front steps when she reached him.

''Thomas. Thomas, thank you.''

''For what?''

''For saving my life.''

"Don't mention it, Pryor."

"Thomas?"

"What?"

"Will you marry me?"

"No."

"I was afraid of that. I've been looking all over for a man who wouldn't care if I've gotten rid of my inheritance. Thomas, Lord Winship told me everything."

Thomas looked at her for a long moment. "Everything?" He observed her standing barefoot in her nightgown. "What exactly are your qualifications?"

"I was a Girl Scout. Upright, forthright, and so forth. I'm honest, kind to children and animals, can cook, garden, and I don't snore."

"A dazzling résumé." She could see that his eyes were bright with tears. She was in his arms before she knew it. A car slowed down so the owner could watch them. Thomas was looking at her as if he'd never let her go. Then he was kissing her as if he'd only now found the mystery, the wonder of life.